NOTHING

The One We Missed

D.M. CHAMBERS

NOTHING BUT
—PRESS—

CONTENTS

NOTHING: THE ONE WE MISSED

CREATED BY: D.M. CHAMBERS

PROLOGUE

It was an average autumn day in Texas—the kind people didn't remark on. A taxi pulled away, leaving Alice outside her childhood church.

The wind tugged at coats and loose paper as if it were impatient.

Alice paused at the church doors, fingers tightening around the strap of her purse. She waited until the slight warmth behind her eyes settled, took a breath, then stepped inside.

Alice's face gave very little away at first glance. Pale. Closed off. Whatever had settled there had been doing so for a long time.

She glanced around the room.

Not many people were there. The pastor. Five strangers who claimed they knew her, but didn't. And her foster brother, Jared.

Jared's eyes flicked briefly to her hoodie. His expression shifted—just enough to register—before he looked away.

He didn't say anything.

Alice was there for her son.

Jesse.

Jesse had died in a car accident five days earlier. He was twelve years old. He'd been riding in the front passenger seat when the collision happened—a head-on impact on a stretch of road Alice had driven a hundred times before. She had been behind the wheel.

That was the version everyone knew.

Jesse had been adventurous. Curious in the way that made him difficult to keep still. He filled rooms without trying to. Alice had spent years bracing herself for the trouble that kind of joy usually found.

She hadn't expected it to end like this.

Alice moved slowly toward the casket, stopping three-quarters of the way there. She stood still, staring at the closed lid. It had been sealed so no one would see what the impact had done to his face. The airbag deployment had caused severe head trauma. There was nothing left to recognize.

Alice had survived with a concussion, bruised ribs, and a dislocated right shoulder that had been reset.

She felt numb. Still, tears slid down her cheeks without warning. To her right, Jared stood quietly, close enough to be present but not close enough to intrude.

Jared stepped toward Alice and lifted a hand as if to touch her shoulder. He stopped himself and let it fall back to his side.

Alice finally reached Jesse's casket. She stood close enough to feel the cold of it, and her lip began to tremble. Memories surfaced without order—the good and the bad, moments that didn't belong together but arrived all the same. None of it mattered. It had ended five days ago.

She still couldn't accept that this was real. That her son was here. That this was where he was supposed to be.

Alice broke.

Her knees gave out and she sank to the floor, one hand pressed against the casket, the other crushing the funeral program until it folded in on itself. Her purse slipped from her shoulder and struck the floor. Something inside caught the light before she could reach for it.

"Why would you take him from me?" she cried,

her voice tearing apart. "He was a good boy. He didn't hurt anyone. He was all I had... he was all I had..."

The words collapsed into themselves.

Jared watched from beside her, his throat tightening. He wiped at his face and breathed through his nose, trying to steady himself before moving.

When he knelt, Alice looked up at him, her breathing uneven.

"I'm glad you came," she said, the words broken by gasps.

He nodded. "Anytime."

He helped her to her feet and guided her back to the pew. Alice leaned against him, her head resting on his shoulder, her arms loosely wrapped around his arm as if letting go might undo her completely.

The service continued. People spoke. Alice spoke. Then it moved outside, toward the burial site.

She rode with Jared. She stayed close to him, physically and otherwise, as if he were the only thing holding her upright.

The burial site sat a short distance from the church, separated by a narrow road and a line of trees that barely moved in the wind. The ground was dry and uneven. Someone had laid out folding chairs, but most people stood instead.

The casket was lowered slowly. The sound of the mechanism working was louder than Alice expected. She kept her eyes fixed on it, afraid that if she looked away, something worse would happen. When it finally settled, the quiet afterward felt heavy, like everyone was waiting for something else to occur.

Nothing did.

The pastor spoke again. Alice didn't listen closely. Words passed through her without staying. She recognized phrases—too young, tragic loss, in God's hands now—but they didn't connect to anything real. They sounded practiced. Safe. She wondered how many times he had said the same things to different families.

When it was over, people began to disperse slowly. Some offered condolences. Others avoided her eyes entirely. A few hugged her, stiff and brief, as if afraid they might break something.

Alice accepted it all without reacting much.

Jared stayed close. He answered questions when she didn't. He thanked people on her behalf. When someone tried to say something reassuring, he nodded for them, gently steering Alice away before the conversation could stretch too long.

Eventually, there was no one left but the workers and the fresh mound of earth.

Alice stood there longer than she needed to.

She didn't cry again. She felt emptied out, as if the earlier collapse had taken everything with it. She watched the dirt settle unevenly, already beginning to look less like a grave and more like disturbed ground.

Jared cleared his throat. "We can go," he said quietly.

She nodded.

On the drive, Alice watched familiar roads pass by—ones she hadn't taken in years. She'd been living across town since her son was born, closer to his school, closer to work. The old house had stayed empty after her parents died. She hadn't planned on going back.

It occurred to her then that the last time she'd lived there, she'd been twelve.

The same age her son had been.

But there was nowhere else that felt appropriate now.

When they reached the house, Jared parked and turned off the engine. For a moment, neither of them moved. Alice stayed in her seat, looking at the house.

It was the same as she remembered.

That, inexplicably, unsettled her.

Jared leaned over, as if deciding whether to speak.

"If you need anything," he said, careful with his words, "just call."

"I know," Alice replied.

She opened the door and stepped out. Jared waited until she was inside before driving away.

The house was quiet when Alice entered. Too quiet. The air felt still, like it had been waiting.

She stood in the doorway for a moment longer than necessary, then closed the door behind her. The latch clicked. The sound stopped too quickly.

As Alice walked farther into her childhood home, the air felt unchanged in a way that unsettled her. Not preserved—suspended.

The smell was familiar enough that her body relaxed before her mind did: dust, old wood, something faintly sweet and long gone. The floorboards creaked where she expected them to, but the sound arrived just late enough to feel rehearsed.

Light entered through the front windows, duller than it should have been for the time of day. Alice glanced at the clock on the wall without thinking. The second hand moved smoothly. The minute hand did not.

The hallway seemed longer than she remembered.

The wallpaper—once white with pale blue flowers—had yellowed unevenly, as though the color had been leeched out in patches. Family photos lined the walls, familiar shapes in familiar frames, exactly where she expected them to be.

She hadn't stopped to look at them. Not really.

She paused in front of one.

Her parents. Herself. A birthday she only vaguely remembered.

Something about the spacing felt wrong.

She leaned closer. Nothing was missing. Nothing had been added. And yet her eyes kept trying to adjust, as though searching for a detail that refused to exist.

She straightened slowly, unsettled in a way she couldn't name, and moved on.

The air grew colder as she moved down the hall —not draft-cold, not physical. The kind of cold that made thoughts feel thinner. Somewhere upstairs, the house shifted. Not a footstep. Not a sound. Just a subtle change, like pressure equalizing behind a sealed door.

She reached the bottom of the stairs and stopped.

For no clear reason, a certainty settled in her chest:

She was not arriving.

She was returning to a process already underway.

I

HOMECOMING

Alice stood at the bottom of the stairs with her left hand resting on the wooden railing, her right pressed lightly to her chest. She remained there longer than she meant to, her gaze fixed on the upper landing.

The door immediately to the left was closed.

Her old bedroom.

Alice stared at it, unmoving, with the uncomfortable sense that something on the other side was already aware of her presence. She couldn't explain the feeling, and she didn't try to. She only knew she wasn't ready to go near it yet.

Instead, she walked to the living room and decided to take a nap on the couch.

Before lying down, she wiped the thin layer of dust from the leather cushions. She clapped the pillows together, sending small clouds of dust into the air. She knew she was doing a poor job, but she didn't care. Fatigue weighed on her too heavily. She just needed rest.

She hadn't had a proper moment of rest since the incident five days ago—the crying, the constant hyper-vigilance. It had drained what little energy she had left.

Alice grabbed a nearby blanket, neatly folded at the edge of the couch, and pulled it over herself, adjusting her position until her shoulder settled comfortably. It didn't take long before she drifted off.

As she slipped into what felt like a deep sleep, she began to dream.

A storm rumbled overhead.

Thoom.

Seven-year-old Alice lay in bed, her covers pulled

up over most of her face. She whimpered softly beneath them. She never liked thunderstorms.

Her father came into the room. He always checked on her when storms started. Alice looked up at him, but she couldn't quite make out his face. Still, she felt his warmth.

"Marilyn," he called down the hallway toward their bedroom. "Can you come in here, please? Alice needs us."

Moments later, heavy, irritated footsteps rushed toward the room.

Marilyn grabbed the doorknob and swung the door open, stumbling inside. Alice couldn't see her mother's face either, but she felt the absence of empathy immediately.

"Oh, for crying out loud, Thomas," Marilyn scoffed, lifting her glass of Cabernet. "She's being such a little bitch."

. . .

Thomas shot her a glare.

"Mari, please. She's seven," he snapped. "Not now. And go easy on the wine."

Marilyn rolled her eyes. "Or what?" she asked mockingly.

Thomas shook his head. "Just go back to the room. We'll talk when I'm done here."

Marilyn smiled faintly, already aware she wouldn't be pushed any further, and turned back toward their bedroom.

Alice's eyes filled with tears. "Why is Mommy so mean to me?" she asked.

Thomas took a breath—slow in, quick out—before answering.

"Your mom's had a bit too much of her... funny juice," he said gently. "She's not very pleasant when she drinks. Not even for your dear old dad."

"But she's always mean to me," Alice said. "I don't know what I do wrong. She always says I'm too much. Or annoying."

Thomas placed a hand on her shoulder.

"You're not too much," he said softly. "You just have more energy than most. Like me. We're not always easy to understand."

Alice nodded.

Suddenly, her father's eyes were the only part of

him she could see clearly—sea-foam green, calm, and kind.

"We're one and the same," Thomas said with a smile.

Alice woke abruptly.

For a moment, she didn't move. Her chest rose and fell too quickly, her heart still racing from the dream. Then she noticed it.

The smell.

Cabernet. Faint, but unmistakable.

She sat up, suddenly alert, and scanned the room. The couch. The coffee table. The darkened corners of the living room. Nothing was out of place. Still, the smell lingered, sharp enough to make her stomach tighten.

Alice swung her legs over the side of the couch and reached for her purse. Her fingers fumbled as she dug inside, checking too quickly, then more carefully. Phone. Wallet. Keys.

No bottle. No glass.

She exhaled, though the relief didn't settle the unease in her chest.

As she straightened, her gaze drifted upward.

The door immediately to the left.

Her childhood bedroom.

It was open.

Alice was certain she hadn't opened it.

She stood there, staring, the smell of wine fading as something colder took its place. She didn't move toward the door. She didn't call out. She only watched it, with the quiet certainty that whatever waited beyond it had been patient.

And it was done waiting.

Alice stood still for a moment, waiting for her breathing to slow.

Her head ached—dull, persistent. Not sharp enough to alarm her, but heavy enough to be irritating. She pressed her fingers briefly to her temple, then let her hand fall. It wasn't worth thinking about yet.

She reached for her purse again.

This time she was slower, more deliberate. She pushed aside her wallet, her keys, the folded receipts she kept meaning to throw away. Her fingers closed around the small orange bottle near the bottom. She turned it once in her hand, then unscrewed the cap and shook out two tablets.

The house was quiet as she walked toward the kitchen.

Each step felt slightly delayed, as though her body were waiting for something to catch up. She ignored the sensation and focused on the cabinets ahead of her. She filled a glass with water and swallowed the pills without looking at them, the familiar bitterness lingering briefly on her tongue.

As she turned back toward the living room, something caught her eye.

The wall.

She stopped.

One of the framed family photos she'd noticed earlier—one she'd paused in front of without realizing how long she'd been standing there—was gone.

Not crooked.

Not fallen.

Gone.

Alice stared at the empty space, her thoughts slow and uncooperative. She tried to remember the photo itself. The colors. The expressions. Who had been standing where.

Nothing came.

She scanned the nearby walls, then the surface of the console table beneath where the frame had been. There was no dust outline. No hook left behind. Just clean, uninterrupted paint.

Her headache pulsed faintly.

Alice looked down at the glass still in her hand, then back at the wall. She told herself she must have been mistaken. That she'd misremembered. That exhaustion had filled in details that hadn't really been there.

She set the glass down and moved on.

She did not go looking for the photo.

Instead, she shook her head and decided to see what was on TV.

Alice headed back into the living room and dropped onto the couch she'd napped on earlier, shifting her weight at the last second to spare her right shoulder. The cushions dipped beneath her weight. She spotted the remote on the coffee table —the same table she vaguely remembered sitting at as a kid, eating her favorite cereal straight from the box.

The memory tugged a small smile from her.

She turned on the television.

It was an old standard set from the nineties—a bulky forty-inch Toshiba that hummed faintly as the screen came to life. The news appeared first.

"Doctor Adams finds new en—"

Click.

"Elmo loves y—"

Click.

"Like I was saying, Maury, Treyvon is my baby's daddy."

Alice clicked her tongue and leaned forward.

"Treyvon, that baby looks nothing like you," she muttered. "That woman is a whole-faced liar."

The host's voice cut in again. "We have your test results for young Treyvon Jr. Treyvon, you are—"

Pew.

The television shut off.

Alice blinked at the blank screen.

"What the hell?" she said, frowning. "I was just about to see that raggedy-ass woman get told Treyvon wasn't Treyvon Jr.'s daddy."

She mashed the power button on the remote. Once. Twice. Again.

Nothing.

She huffed, tossed the remote aside, and threw her left hand up.

"Fuckin' old TVs," she muttered. "I swear."

As her reflection stared back at her from the darkened screen, something behind her caught her attention.

The wall.

The framed photo that had been missing earlier was there again.

Or—maybe it had never been gone.

Alice frowned slightly, her certainty wavering as she stared at the reflection. The thought settled uncomfortably in her chest, reshaping itself into something easier to accept.

Maybe she'd imagined it.

Either way, it felt like too much to dwell on in the moment.

Instead, Alice reached for her purse, intending to find her phone so she could text Jared. Her fingers brushed past loose items—receipts, keys—before catching on folded paper.

She froze.

Jesse's funeral program.

It was creased down the middle, worn soft from being handled too many times. The sight of it sent a sudden rush through her chest, sharp and unwelcome. Grief surged back in all at once, heavier than she expected.

She realized, distantly, that she'd been starting to feel almost normal.

The nap. The television. The quiet routine of the house. For a brief moment, they had pulled her away from real life—away from the weight of what had happened.

Now it came rushing back.

Alice closed her eyes and exhaled slowly, the program still clutched in her hand.

The tears came again.

She broke down again—but this time there was no one to turn to. No one to hold onto. No one to absorb the weight of it with her.

Alice felt the loneliness settle fully, heavy and undeniable.

"Why did you take him?" she cried, her voice breaking. "He was innocent. Jesse was innocent... dammit."

Her breath hitched. The words that followed tore out of her before she could stop them.

"It should've been me that day," she sobbed. "Not him. Oh God—why?"

Her legs gave out.

Alice collapsed to the floor, the grief pulling her down with the same certainty as gravity. Tears streamed freely, splashing onto the dusty hardwood beneath her. She pressed her forehead down, shoulders shaking, the house offering nothing in return.

The house didn't react.

It didn't creak. It didn't shift.

It simply stayed the same, as if grief were just another sound it had learned to ignore.

She wiped her face and looked up, blinking.

The light through the window had thinned. She tried to remember how long she'd been on the floor, but the thought slid away before it settled.

She pushed herself upright, favoring her left side as she stood. A dull ache flared through her right shoulder—sharp enough to make her pause, not sharp enough to stop her.

She tugged the sleeves of her hoodie down over her wrists before moving.

From the staircase, a soft glow reached the walls above. It came from the hallway upstairs.

Her parents' bedroom.

Alice didn't move.

She turned toward the stairs. Before climbing, she rested her left hand on the banister again. The wood felt the same as it had earlier—smooth where hands had worn it down over time, cooler along the underside. She let her fingers linger, not searching for anything in particular.

Whatever she'd felt before didn't return.

After a moment, she climbed.

The steps were slower than she expected, her legs still unsteady, each one taken with care. She avoided pulling herself up with her right arm, keeping it close to her body as she went. The house remained quiet, unchanged.

At the top, she passed her old bedroom. The door stood open.

She didn't slow down.

The light farther down the hall held steady, warmer than it should have been. It didn't flicker or dim. It suggested a later hour—one the windows below hadn't agreed with.

She paused.

The door at the end of the hall wasn't fully closed.

A thin line of light cut across the floor, stopping just short of her feet. Alice stood there long enough to register the difference—between what she'd seen downstairs and what the hallway insisted on now.

The effort to reconcile it faded before it finished.

She shifted her weight, her shoulder twinging

again—a quiet reminder of the accident, of the way her body hadn't entirely caught up to the idea of surviving.

Alice turned away from her parents' bedroom door.

The light did not change.

The house accepted the decision without comment.

Alice went back downstairs.

She didn't rush. She didn't linger either. Just moved, step by step, as if following a path she'd already agreed to without remembering when.

The living room was dimmer than before. Evening had settled in quietly, the light outside thinning into something gray and indistinct. She lowered herself onto the couch again, adjusting her weight automatically so her shoulder wouldn't complain.

It didn't.

Or if it did, it wasn't loud enough to matter.

Her stomach tightened—not hunger, exactly. More like absence. She pulled her phone from her purse and unlocked it, the screen lighting her face in soft, artificial blue.

A delivery app opened. She scrolled without thinking, past food that looked too bright, too heavy. She stopped on something simple and stared at it longer than necessary.

She added it to her cart.

The television turned on.

The screen flared to life in front of her, washing the room in pale light.

Alice startled, just enough to lift her gaze. Her first thought arrived fully formed.

I must've sat on the remote.

She shifted on the couch, checking beneath her leg, then leaned forward to look at the coffee table.

The remote was there.

Exactly where she'd left it.

She frowned, irritation surfacing before fear could catch up. "Seriously?" she muttered.

The screen held on an image she didn't recognize. No channel logo. No sound. Just a frozen frame, as if the TV had been paused without her input.

Alice reached out with her left hand and pressed the power button.

The screen went dark.

She waited.

Nothing followed.

She exhaled and looked back down at her phone. The delivery app dimmed, a small message asking if she was still there.

She tapped it awake and finished the order.

The room settled again. Quiet. Ordinary.

Alice leaned back against the couch and closed her eyes, just for a moment.

The house stayed exactly as it was.

The knock came sooner than she expected.

Alice stirred, unsure how long she'd been sitting there. The light outside had dimmed further, the sky settling into a flat gray that gave no hint of time. She grabbed her purse and moved toward the front door, adjusting her grip so the bag wouldn't tug at her shoulder.

The delivery driver didn't linger. A paper bag was passed into her hands, warm through the bottom, the exchange brief and wordless. Alice muttered a thank-you and closed the door behind her.

The latch clicked.

She turned the lock.

From the living room, the television began to play sound.

Alice froze.

Not static. Not feedback.

Voices.

Muffled at first, then clearer—overlapping dialogue, a familiar cadence. The rhythm of a show she might have watched before, but couldn't place.

She didn't move.

After a moment, she set the food down slowly on the console table and walked back toward the living room.

The television was on.

The screen was black.

No menu. No input label. No glow at the edges. Just a dark, reflective surface filled with sound that didn't belong to it.

A laugh track rolled faintly through the speakers.

Alice stared at the screen, her reflection faint against the black.

Her heart didn't race. Not yet.

She pressed the power button on the remote.

The sound stopped instantly.

The screen remained black.

Alice stood there a moment longer than necessary, waiting for something else to happen.

Nothing did.

She exhaled and shook her head once, as if clearing water from her ears.

"Okay," she said quietly.

She picked up the food and carried it into the kitchen.

Behind her, the television stayed dark and silent.

It didn't turn back on.

Not yet.

Alice stood in front of the television, remote loose in her left hand.

She pressed the power button.

The screen flickered, then filled with color.

A daytime talk show. The same set as before. The host mid-sentence, mouth moving in time with an audience reaction she couldn't hear.

No sound.

She frowned and pressed the volume button.

Nothing.

She pressed it again. Held it down. The on-screen bar climbed steadily until it maxed out.

Still nothing.

Alice angled the remote toward the TV and clicked again, irritation creeping in. "Come on," she muttered.

The host laughed silently. Applause rippled across the audience in complete, soundless unison.

Her stomach tightened.

She took a step closer.

Then another.

The room felt quieter the nearer she got, like the air itself was thinning. She leaned in, head tilting slightly, as if proximity might solve what technology wouldn't.

She was close enough now to see her reflection layered faintly over the screen.

SLAM.

The sound detonated behind her.

Alice flinched hard, her shoulder protesting as she spun halfway around.

The door to her childhood bedroom had slammed shut.

Not creaked.

Not drifted.

Shut.

The house went still again.

Alice stood frozen between the television and the hallway, heart pounding now—loud enough to drown out the silence the TV had left behind.

Slowly, she turned back toward the screen.

The show continued, picture-perfect and mute.

Waiting.

Alice stood in front of the television, the remote warm in her left hand.

She pressed the power button.

The screen filled with color.

The talk show snapped back to life at full volume.

Alice winced, startled more by the suddenness than the noise itself. The host's voice boomed through the speakers, the laugh track crashing in behind it, loud enough to feel disproportionate to the quiet of the house.

"Jesus—" she muttered, jabbing the volume button.

The sound dropped a few notches. Still loud. She lowered it again until it settled into something tolerable.

She exhaled, shoulders loosening.

"Of course," she said to no one. "It's old."

She glanced at the set—the bulky frame, the faint hum beneath the audio. It had always done things like that. Cut out. Spiked. Behaved like it had a personality.

The show played normally now. Picture and

sound in sync. The room felt fuller with it on, less hollow.

Alice set the remote down and picked up the food bag again, the warmth grounding in her hands.

She carried it into the kitchen, telling herself she'd eat and then lie down for a bit.

Behind her, the television continued without issue.

For now.

Alice sat at the small kitchen table with the takeout spread in front of her, the paper containers opened but untouched for a moment longer than they should've been.

The television murmured from the living room. Not loud. Just present. A steady wash of voices and canned laughter that filled the house without asking for attention.

She took a few bites. The food was warm, decent enough. She chewed mechanically, barely tasting it. Her eyes drifted toward the doorway, unfocused, listening without listening as the show carried on.

Someone on the TV said something she didn't catch. The audience laughed anyway.

Halfway through the meal, her chest tightened.

There was no thought attached to it at first— just a familiar pressure settling behind her ribs. She swallowed and tried to keep eating. Her hands shook as she set the fork down.

She stared at the table.

He would've liked this.

The thought arrived fully formed, uninvited. Not sharp. Not dramatic. Just heavy. Like it had been waiting its turn.

Her throat burned. Alice pressed her lips together, willing the feeling to pass.

It didn't.

Tears slipped free, quiet and steady. She covered her mouth, shoulders folding inward as her breathing caught. The sound she made was small, almost embarrassed by its own existence.

The television kept talking.

She cried at the table until her head ached and her chest felt hollow. At some point, she rested her forehead against her folded arms. The surface was cool beneath her skin.

Her sobs softened. Slowed.

Grief settled into exhaustion.

Alice cried herself to sleep.

Alice dreamed she was seven years old.

She stood barefoot at the far end of the upstairs hallway, the wooden floor cool beneath her feet. The house looked brighter than she remembered—cleaner, warmer. The walls held the faint glow of evening light, and the air smelled like dust and something sweet she couldn't name.

From the room at the end of the hall, she heard her father's voice.

He sounded happy.

Not loud. Not drunk. Just easy—talking the way he did when he was relaxed, when the day had gone well. He was speaking to someone, laughing softly between sentences.

Alice smiled.

She took a step forward.

The sound of her feet on the wood followed her, light and quick. She walked faster now, drawn by the sound of his voice, the comfort of knowing he was there. The door to her parents' bedroom was cracked open, a thin line of warm light spilling into the hallway.

She slowed as she got closer.

Something about the sound wasn't right.

Her father's voice continued, steady and kind— but the timing felt off. He laughed a beat too late. His words overlapped themselves slightly, as if the conversation were looping around something she couldn't hear.

Alice stopped just short of the door.

Inside, the light shifted.

The door began to open.

Not all at once. Just a little more—slow enough that she could tell it was moving.

Small fingers curled around the edge of the door.

They tightened, pale knuckles pressing against the wood as the door opened wider.

Alice's smile faltered.

A face appeared in the gap.

Jesse.

Not as he'd looked when he died.

Younger. Eight, maybe. His hair still falling into his eyes the way she used to trim unevenly. His expression was calm. Familiar. Like he'd been standing there for a while.

He looked at her.

"Mom," he said.

Her heart lurched—not in fear, but in recognition.

Behind him, her father's voice continued, still talking, still warm, as if nothing had changed.

Jesse didn't move aside.

He didn't smile.

"You're not supposed to be here yet," he said gently.

Alice tried to speak. Tried to step forward.

The hallway felt heavier all at once, the air thickening as though the house itself were holding its breath.

Jesse's fingers tightened on the door.

"Go back," he said. Not unkindly. "He's busy."

The door began to close.

Alice woke with a sharp intake of breath, her heart pounding, her chest tight.

For a moment, she lay still, staring into the dark, the echo of her father's voice fading too slowly from her ears.

The house was quiet.

No footsteps. No voices.

Just the steady, unbroken silence of wood and walls and closed doors.

Alice turned onto her side and pulled the blanket closer, as if that might be enough.

She did not dream again.

2

UNATTENDED

A lice woke to light.

Not the gradual kind. Not morning easing its way in. It was already there—flat and bright, pressing through the windows as if it had been waiting for her to open her eyes.

She frowned and turned her head toward the living room window.

Sunlight filled the space, warm and unmistakable. The kind that belonged to late morning or early afternoon. It painted the wood floors in long, pale shapes and caught on the edges of furniture she didn't remember falling asleep near.

Alice lay still for a moment, disoriented.

Her body felt heavy, stiff from sleeping wrong.

Her shoulder tugged faintly as she shifted, then settled again. The house was quiet—no television, no
hum of appliances, no distant noise from outside.

She reached for her phone.

The screen lit up.

8:12 a.m.

Alice stared at the number.

That didn't make sense.

She scrolled instinctively, checking the date. The
day. Everything was correct. Monday. Morning. Too
early for the light she was seeing.

Her phone vibrated in her hand.

Jared.

She hesitated before answering, her thumb hovering a fraction of a second too long.

"Hey," she said when she picked up, her voice
rough.

"Hey," Jared replied. He sounded awake. Alert.
Normal. "I just wanted to check on you. You okay?"

Alice glanced around the room as he spoke. The
couch. The table. The blanket pulled around her
shoulders. Nothing looked disturbed. Nothing
looked wrong.

"I think so," she said. The words came out automatically. "I just woke up."

"Did you sleep?" he asked.

She thought of the dream. Her father's voice.
Jesse standing in the doorway.

"I guess," she said. "It doesn't really feel like it."

There was a pause on the other end of the line—not heavy, just careful.

"You want me to come by later?" Jared asked. "I can bring coffee or something."

Alice's gaze drifted toward the staircase without her meaning to. The hallway above was bright now, evenly lit, every door closed.

"No," she said quickly. Then, softer, "Not yet."

"Okay," he said. "Just... call me if you need anything."

"I will."

They hung up.

Alice set the phone down and sat up slowly, letting her feet touch the floor. The wood was cool beneath her skin.

She stood, steadying herself, and looked once more at the sunlight spilling through the windows.

It felt too complete.

Like the house had already moved on without her.

Alice rubbed her face and headed for the kitchen, telling herself she was tired. That grief did strange things to time. That old houses held heat differently.

Behind her, the upstairs hallway remained quiet.

Every door stayed closed.

And that should have been comforting.

Alice stood and stretched slowly, letting the stiffness work itself out. Her shoulder complained faintly as she rolled it, then settled again. The light in the room still felt wrong—too complete, too awake—but she pushed the thought aside.

She glanced at the kitchen table.

The takeout containers sat where she'd left them. Open. Congealed. The smell had changed— not rotten, just off. Cold in a way that made her stomach turn.

She stared at the food longer than necessary.

"What a waste," she muttered.

Carefully, she gathered the containers and carried them to the trash, avoiding looking too closely as she dumped them out. She hated throwing food away. Always had. It felt careless. Wrong. But she wasn't about to risk getting sick on top of everything else.

She washed her hands and dried them, then pulled out her phone.

Groceries.

The word anchored her. Something normal. Something that made sense.

She sat back down and opened the delivery app, scrolling more deliberately this time. Coffee first. Grounds, filters. Creamer. Then the basics—eggs, bread, fruit that would last. Soup. Frozen meals she could ignore if she needed to. Enough for a week. Maybe a little more.

She hesitated, thumb hovering, then added a few extra items. Just in case.

When she placed the order, a confirmation screen popped up with an estimated delivery window.

2–3 hours.

"Fine," she said quietly.

She set the phone on the counter and filled the kettle, then stopped. No coffee yet. She'd shower first. Let the day start properly.

Upstairs, the bathroom felt warmer than she expected. Steam built quickly, fogging the mirror as soon as the water heated. Alice stepped under the spray and closed her eyes, letting the water beat against her shoulders and back.

She didn't rush.

She stood there longer than usual, breathing steadily, letting her thoughts drift without latching onto anything sharp. The sound of the water filled the space completely, blotting out the rest of the house.

At some point, she rested her forehead against the cool tile and stayed there, eyes closed, until the heat soaked into her skin and her muscles finally loosened.

When she turned the water off, the bathroom felt strangely quiet.

She reached for her towel and glanced at her phone on the counter.

The screen was black.

She frowned and tapped it once. Nothing.

Again. Still nothing.

"That's weird," she said.

She plugged it into the charger by the sink and waited.

No vibration. No battery symbol.

Her chest tightened slightly—not panic, just irritation. She dried off quickly, wrapped herself in the towel, and headed downstairs.

The house was bright.

Brighter than before.

Sunlight flooded the living room now, sharp and high, casting clear shapes across the wood floor. It looked like afternoon.

Alice stopped at the bottom of the stairs and stared.

That wasn't possible.

She hurried to the front window and pulled the curtain back.

The sky was pale and open. The sun sat higher than it should have.

Her heart picked up speed.

She turned toward the kitchen, then froze.

Paper bags lined the front porch.

Groceries.

They sat neatly against the door, undisturbed. Condensation darkened the bottoms of a few bags. A carton of milk peeked out from the top, wet to the touch when she lifted it.

"No," she whispered.

She dragged the bags inside one by one, setting them on the counter. Cold items first. Too warm. Not warm enough to be safe. The frozen meals were soft at the edges.

She checked the receipt.

Delivered over an hour ago.

Alice swallowed hard and looked back toward the stairs, then at the dead phone still plugged in uselessly by the sink.

Her coffee sat unmade. Her food ruined. Time— gone.

She leaned against the counter, suddenly exhausted.

"I was just in the shower," she said aloud.

The house did not respond.

Outside, the light remained steady.

And nothing about it felt rushed.

Alice stood at the kitchen counter, staring down at the grocery bags she'd dragged inside.

She opened them one by one, slower now. Methodical. Milk first—too warm. She tipped the carton gently, watching the liquid slosh inside, then set it aside. Yogurt next. Soft around the edges. The frozen meals bent under her fingers, no longer rigid.

She sorted what she could save from what she couldn't, lining items up in neat rows along the counter. Bread. Canned soup. Dry pasta. A bag of apples she turned in her hand before setting them with the rest of the keep pile.

The discard pile still grew.

She carried the ruined items to the trash in two trips and returned to the counter without looking back.

Her phone buzzed.

Alice froze, then glanced at the screen.

1 new voicemail — Jared

She didn't open it.

Her eyes dropped instead to the battery indicator.

67%.

The number sat there, steady and unremarkable.

She stared at it for a moment, then unlocked the phone and opened the grocery app again. Milk. Frozen meals. Refrigerated basics. Only what she'd had to throw out.

She placed the order and set the phone down.

Coffee next.

She scooped the grounds into the filter, filled the machine, and pressed the button. It hummed to life. The smell spread quickly, familiar and grounding.

She poured herself a cup and took a sip.

Grimaced.

"Too strong," she muttered, though she didn't pour it out.

Mug in hand, she moved through the house, cleaning as she went. Wiped the counters. Straightened the couch cushions. Gathered stray items and put them back where they belonged.

The house seemed to accept the effort.

Light slid across the wood floors as she worked. The air felt clearer once the windows were cracked open. Even the television faded into the background, its low murmur no longer demanding attention.

At some point, she realized her shoulder hadn't bothered her in a while.

That felt like progress.

When she finished, Alice leaned against the kitchen counter and took another sip of coffee. Still bitter. Still hot.

She drank it anyway.

Her phone sat nearby, screen dark. The voicemail untouched.

The house remained quiet.

For now.

The grocery delivery arrived right on time.

Alice noticed the car pulling up through the front window and felt a small, surprising sense of relief. She grabbed her keys and opened the door before the driver could knock.

"Hey," she said, stepping aside. "I can help."

He looked a little startled, then smiled. "Thanks. Makes it easier."

The driver carried the groceries to the front porch, and Alice took it from there—quick, efficient, unremarkable. Cold items felt properly chilled. Frozen meals were solid again. Everything smelled clean and fresh.

Nothing was wrong.

The driver nodded once, checked his phone, and left without lingering.

Alice shut the door and locked it.

She unpacked the groceries immediately, moving with practiced familiarity. Milk in the fridge. Yogurt beside it. Frozen meals stacked neatly in the freezer. She took her time, double-checking dates, feeling reassured by how ordinary everything was.

When she finished, the kitchen looked right again.

She leaned against the counter and exhaled.

Only then did she notice her phone.

It sat where she'd left it earlier, screen dark. Alice picked it up and tapped the voicemail icon.

Jared's name sat at the top.

She hesitated.

Then she pressed play.

"Hey," Jared said, his voice lower than usual. "Uh... I stopped by earlier. I rang the doorbell, but no one answered."

Alice frowned.

"I didn't want to freak you out or anything," he continued. "I figured maybe you were in the shower. Or asleep. But... yeah. It was weird. It was like no one was home."

There was a brief pause.

"Anyway. Just wanted to make sure you're okay. Call me when you get this."

The voicemail ended.

Alice lowered the phone slowly.

I would have heard that, she thought immediately.

The certainty came fast. Automatic. The doorbell echoed through the house. It always had. Even from upstairs.

She stared at the phone, then shook her head once.

"Yeah," she said quietly. "I would've heard it."

She walked to the front door and opened it.

The porch was empty.

Alice stepped back inside and pressed the doorbell.

The sound rang out instantly—clear, sharp, unmistakable. It traveled cleanly through the house, bouncing off the wood floors, carrying down the hall and up the stairs.

There was no delay.

No muffling.

No way to miss it.

Alice stood there, listening as the sound faded.

Her stomach tightened.

She pressed it again.

The bell rang just as loudly.

She let her hand fall away and backed up a step, eyes fixed on the door.

The house was quiet again.

Too quiet for something that should have announced itself.

Alice stood in the kitchen a moment longer after the doorbell test, then shook her head once and picked up her phone.

She hit call.

Jared answered on the second ring.

"Hey," he said. He sounded relieved. "You okay?"

"Yeah," Alice said. "Yeah, I'm fine. Sorry—I was busy earlier."

There was a pause. Not awkward. Just checking.

"I didn't mean to freak you out," he said. "I just wanted to make sure you were actually there."

"I was," she replied. The words came easily. Too easily. "I am."

"Good." He exhaled. "Good."

They talked for a few minutes after that. Nothing heavy. Groceries. The house. How she was holding up. Alice kept her answers short but honest enough to sound normal.

"Do you want to come by?" she asked finally. "You don't have to stay long."

Another pause. This one lasted a beat longer.

"Yeah," Jared said. "Okay. I can do that."

When the call ended, Alice set the phone down

and moved through the house again, this time toward the study.

The room sat just off the hallway—quiet, darker than the rest of the first floor. Built-in shelves lined the walls, most of them still filled. Old books. Binders. Things her parents had kept because they didn't know where else to put them.

The cabinet beneath the window creaked softly when she opened it.

The bottle was still there.

Cabernet.

Her mother's handwriting was faint on the label —just a date and a small star in the corner. Alice turned it once in her hands, feeling the weight of it, the familiarity. For a moment, the room felt closer than it should have.

She hesitated.

Then she took it to the kitchen.

The cork came out with a muted pop. She poured herself a glass and took a sip.

It tasted exactly how she remembered.

She grimaced anyway.

"Still awful," she muttered, and took another sip.

Then another.

Not because she wanted to drink—but because her chest felt tight, and the act of doing something felt better than standing still.

She heard a car outside a few minutes later.

Alice looked through the front window.

Jared stood by the curb, keys in hand.

She opened the door.

"Hey," she said.

He smiled, but it didn't quite reach his eyes. He stayed where he was.

"I'm good out here," he said. "If that's okay."

Alice frowned slightly. "You don't want to come in?"

Jared glanced past her, just briefly. Not searching. Not staring.

"I don't know," he said. "It's stupid. I just... don't feel right."

The words landed heavier than he seemed to intend.

"That's fine," Alice said quickly. "Really."

They talked there for a bit instead—on the porch, the evening air cooling around them. About nothing important. About everything that didn't need to be said yet.

When he left, Alice stood in the doorway and watched his car disappear down the street.

She closed the door and locked it.

The house settled.

The Cabernet sat on the counter behind her, half-full.

She didn't look at it.

She walked to the fridge instead.

Alice reheated one of the frozen meals she'd just put away.

The microwave hummed, the familiar rattle filling the kitchen. She leaned against the counter while it ran, eyes unfocused, listening more to the sound than the time. When it finished, she carried the tray into the living room and set it on the coffee table.

She sat on the couch and turned the television on.

Some daytime program she didn't recognize filled the screen. Voices overlapped. Laughter came too quickly. She didn't change it.

She ate slowly, barely tasting anything. The food was fine—hot, properly cooked, exactly what it was supposed to be. She took a few bites, watched the screen, took a few more.

At some point, her fork paused halfway to her mouth.

She wasn't watching the TV anymore.

Her thoughts had slipped sideways, looping back to things she hadn't meant to think about. The quiet after the funeral. The way the house had smelled when she first walked in. How easily the day had started to feel almost normal.

This shouldn't feel normal, she thought.

Her chest tightened without warning.

Alice set the fork down and pressed her lips together, staring at the television as her eyes blurred. The sound continued, cheerful and indifferent. Someone on-screen laughed at something that wasn't funny.

Her shoulders shook once.

Then again.

She tried to steady herself, to breathe through it, but the feeling came faster this time—hot and heavy, pressing up from somewhere she hadn't braced for.

Tears spilled over.

She leaned forward, elbows on her knees, one hand covering her mouth as she cried quietly. The food sat untouched in front of her, steam long gone.

Nothing specific had triggered it.

No memory. No sound. No thought she could point to.

Just the accumulation of everything she'd been holding together all day.

The crying wore her down quickly. It always did.

When it finally eased, Alice wiped her face with the sleeve of her hoodie and sat back against the couch, exhausted. The television murmured on. The house stayed still around her.

She didn't turn the TV off.

She didn't clean up the plate.

She just closed her eyes.

Alice stirred.

Not fully awake—just enough for the room to

shift, the television's noise blurring into a low, distant hum. Her eyes fluttered open, unfocused, the ceiling above her unfamiliar for half a second before memory slid back into place.

The couch.

The house.

Her right hand felt warm.

Alice frowned faintly, still heavy with sleep.

Small fingers curled around hers.

Her breath caught.

She turned her head slowly, the movement sluggish, as if the air itself resisted her. Jesse stood beside the couch, just close enough to touch her. Not as he'd been lately—taller, louder, always moving—but smaller. Seven, maybe. Eight.

The age before everything had gotten complicated.

He didn't look hurt.

He didn't look scared.

He just looked at her, eyes lowered, holding her hand like he used to when he was tired and didn't want to say it.

"I'm sorry," Alice whispered.

The words slipped out without thought, without shape. An apology she'd been carrying too long to keep track of.

Jesse squeezed her hand once.

Then the warmth faded.

Alice's eyes closed again, her grip loosening as

sleep reclaimed her. The television continued murmuring softly. The plate on the coffee table sat untouched, forgotten.

The house held its breath.

Let her go.

Alice was seven again.

The hallway stretched longer than it should have, the wood floor smooth beneath her bare feet. Light spilled from the end of the hall — her parents' bedroom — the door cracked open wider than before.

She could hear her father's voice.

Warm. Animated. Talking to someone she couldn't see.

Relief flooded her chest. She started toward it.

As she got closer, her mother's voice joined in. Sharp at first. Irritated. The familiar edge Alice had learned to measure herself against.

They were arguing.

The words overlapped, indistinct, rising and falling in rhythm rather than meaning. The door creaked open another inch.

Then something shifted.

The argument dissolved into laughter.

Not natural laughter. Too loud. Too sudden.

Her mother laughed until it cracked into sobbing. Her father cried openly, shoulders shaking — but his laughter never stopped. The sounds braided together, joy and grief indistinguishable, filling the hallway until Alice couldn't tell which emotion she was hearing anymore.

She froze.

The door opened wider.

Hands appeared first — gripping the edge of the doorframe from inside. Fingers flexing, knuckles whitening, as if bracing against something unseen.

Then—

CLAP.

The sound exploded through the hallway.

A voice followed it. Not her parents'. Not human.

"WAKE UP."

CLAP.

Alice jolted.

CLAP.

"WAKE UP."

Alice jolted.

Her eyes flew open, her breath tearing in as she sucked in air too fast. The living room swam back into focus—the couch beneath her, the low glow of the television, the familiar shapes of the house set-tling back into place.

Her heart hammered against her ribs.

For a moment, she didn't move.

The dream clung to her, fragments of sound and feeling still pressed against the inside of her skull. Laughter tangled with crying. The sharp command echoing louder than it should have.

Wake up.

She swallowed and shifted on the couch, grounding herself in the present. The television murmured on, unchanged. Nothing in the room looked disturbed.

Alice's stomach growled.

The sound startled her.

She glanced down at the coffee table.

Her plate sat where she'd left it.

She reached for her fork and took a bite without really looking, grateful for the normalcy of the motion, the simple certainty of eating something real.

The taste hit her halfway through chewing.

Wrong.

Her body reacted before her mind caught up.

Alice gagged and spat the food back onto the plate, breath hitching as she stared down.

The meal was no longer just cold.

Gray-green fuzz spread across it in thick patches, crawling over the surface, threaded with darker veins. Mold bloomed along the edges, dense and unmistakable, as if it had been sitting out for days.

Her fork clattered from her hand.

Alice stared, frozen, her pulse roaring in her ears.

She hadn't fallen asleep that long.

She knew she hadn't.

The television laughed at something in the background.

Alice pushed herself back against the couch, eyes

locked on the plate, her mouth tasting sour and wrong.

Nothing else in the room had changed.

Just the food.

Just enough.

3

PLAYBACK

Alice shoved the plate away from her.
The food slid across the coffee table and bumped softly against the edge, stopping just short of falling. She watched it for a moment, breath shallow, waiting for something to change.

Nothing did.

No sour smell.

No creeping discoloration.

Just half-eaten food cooling in the open air, ordinary again.

Her stomach twisted anyway.

Alice leaned back against the couch and pressed

her palms into the cushions, grounding herself in the fabric, the weight of her body, the low murmur of the television still playing. The room looked exactly the same as it had before. Too cooperative. Too willing to pretend nothing had happened.

She wiped her mouth with the sleeve of her hoodie and looked up.

That was when she noticed a VCR.

It sat beneath the television, tucked neatly into the stand as if it had always been there. Black plastic. Dusty, but not abandoned. A faint red glow shone through the display on its face.

2:17

Alice frowned.

She didn't remember owning a VCR. She was sure she would have noticed it before—at some point, anyway. But the thought slipped away as quickly as it came, replaced by a quieter assumption.

Maybe it was always there.

Her gaze dropped to the slot.

There was already a tape inside.

Two more lay on the floor beside the stand, slightly crooked, like someone had set them down and meant to come back.

Alice hesitated, then reached for the remote.

The machine responded instantly. The television flickered—static for half a second—then resolved into color.

A date appeared in the corner of the screen.

MAY 7, 1997

The footage wobbled as the camera adjusted. Sunlight flooded the frame, bright and warm, washing over a backyard Alice recognized immediately.

Her backyard.

A child darted into view, laughing, the hem of a little red dress bouncing against her knees as she spun in a clumsy circle. Someone behind the camera laughed too—deep, unguarded, familiar.

Her father's voice.

Alice's breath hitched.

She sank down onto the floor without realizing she'd moved, settling cross-legged directly in front of the television. The picture wasn't perfect. The colors were slightly washed, the sound thin at the edges. But it was real. Sharper than memory. Less forgiving.

She watched herself—five years old, hair pulled back unevenly—run toward the camera before veering off again. Marilyn appeared at the edge of the frame, calling her name, laughing as she chased after her. Her blouse was loose and wrinkled, one sleeve slipping down her arm as she ran. Her hair wasn't done the way Alice remembered it usually being—pulled back too quickly, strands escaping at her temples—but her face was open, flushed with exertion and joy.

Everyone sounded happy.

Uncomplicated.

Alice pressed a hand to her mouth as tears spilled over, hot and sudden. Not fear. Not sadness.

Relief.

She remembered this day. The heat. The grass sticking to her legs. Her father filming even though no one had asked him to. The feeling that nothing bad was waiting around the corner.

She laughed softly through her tears, shaking her head as if the screen might see her.

The tape played on, indifferent.

Then it ended.

The screen went blue.

Behind her, the study door creaked open.

The sound was small—just the soft complaint of old hinges—but it cut cleanly through the quiet. Alice glanced over her shoulder.

The hallway beyond was empty.

She stayed where she was for a moment, heart slowing, then pushed herself to her feet. Her legs felt stiff, like she'd been sitting longer than she thought.

She glanced at the VCR clock.

11:42

Alice frowned.

That couldn't be right.

She pulled her phone from her pocket and checked the screen.

11:42.

Her stomach tightened. She crossed to the window and pulled the curtain back just enough to look outside. Late-morning light spilled across the yard at a clean, undeniable angle. Bright. Honest.

She let the curtain fall.

"Okay," she murmured, more to herself than anything else.

The study door remained open.

Alice stepped into the hallway, drawn less by curiosity than by the quiet pull of familiarity. Her mother had always kept wine in the study. She remembered it suddenly—not as a new thought, but as something already lived. She'd grabbed a glass earlier, before Jared came, from the rack beside the bookshelf, tucked out of sight where it had always been.

The room felt different now that she was standing in it.

Not wrong. Just... contained.

She took the time to actually look around. The desk. The shelves. The corners she hadn't paid attention to earlier. That was when she noticed the small bookshelf tucked against the back right wall.

VHS tapes filled it.

Neatly arranged. Spines facing out. Older ones on the left, newer on the right. Chronological. Responsible.

Alice's throat tightened.

She didn't take long. Just one tape, slipped carefully from its place. She turned it over in her hands, then headed back toward the living room.

The food still sat on the coffee table, untouched.

She stepped around it without looking down.

Alice slid the new tape into the VCR and sat back on the floor, close to the screen again.

The clock glowed softly beneath the television.

She pressed play.

Then stopped.

Alice frowned at herself and reached for the remote again, thumb hovering. The image on the screen froze—her younger self caught mid-motion, sunlight glinting off the edge of the frame.

She exhaled.

This didn't need to feel like this.

Not this early.

Alice stood and went back into the kitchen. The wine was still there, right where she'd left it earlier—glass untouched near the sink, the bottle beside it, half-full. She'd forgotten about it completely.

For a second, she just looked at it.

Then she picked both up.

She carried them back into the living room carefully, like she was settling in for something intentional. The bottle went on the floor beside the couch, the glass within easy reach. She lowered herself onto the wooden floor, sitting close to the television again, the cool boards firm beneath her.

A small smile tugged at her mouth.

A stroll down memory lane, she thought.

Alice lifted the glass, took a slow sip, and felt the tightness in her chest ease.

Only then did she press play.

The screen flickered.

For a moment, nothing happened—just a soft hum from the VCR, the faint hiss of static bleeding through the speakers. Then the traffic of color resolved into motion.

Another backyard.

Not the same one.

This one was smaller, tighter. The fence sat closer to the camera, the grass uneven and patchy. The sun hung lower in the sky, its light warmer, more orange than before.

Alice leaned forward.

A child stepped into frame—older this time. Seven, maybe eight. Hair longer, pulled back with less care. The camera dipped slightly as the person holding it laughed.

Her father again.

She recognized the sound instantly. Not the laugh itself, but the breath that came after it—the way he always seemed slightly out of breath, even when he wasn't doing anything at all.

"Hold still," he said, amused. "You're not even in the shot."

Alice smiled despite herself.

On-screen, she rolled her eyes and planted her feet, hands on her hips. The dress was different. Blue this time. Wrinkled at the hem. She remembered this one too. Not the day exactly, but the feeling of it—heat, impatience, wanting to be grown already.

The timestamp blinked in the corner of the screen.

AUG 12, 1999

The tape played on without interruption. No jumps. No distortion. Just another piece of her life, recorded and preserved without knowing it would ever be needed.

Alice reached for the wine without looking, lifted the glass, and took a small sip. The taste grounded her, softened the edge of the room. Her shoulders eased.

She shifted, settling in more comfortably.

At some point, she realized her legs had gone numb.

She glanced down, flexed her toes, then looked back up at the screen.

The VCR clock read 2:17.

That didn't make sense.

She could have sworn it had read something else

a minute ago. Alice frowned and pulled her phone from her pocket.

2:17.

Her smile faltered.

She glanced toward the window, then back at the television. The light in the room still felt right—bright enough to be afternoon, not late morning. She let out a slow breath and told herself she was overthinking it.

The tape ended.

The screen went blue.

Alice didn't move right away.

She stared at the blank screen, the echo of her father's laughter still ringing faintly in her ears, the wine warm in her stomach.

The day felt... compressed.

Like she'd folded something too many times.

She shook her head once, as if to clear it, and reached for the next tape. Inserted it into the VCR and hit play.

The screen flickered.

Static hissed softly, then thinned, giving way to color. The image steadied on a front door Alice recognized immediately—white paint chipped near the handle, the brass knob catching the light.

A date blinked into place in the corner.

SEP 9, 1998

Alice smiled.

The camera shifted, unsteady, then settled as her

father laughed behind it. His voice sounded closer than before, breathier, like he was crouched down to keep her in frame.

"Okay," he said. "You ready?"

A younger Alice stood in the doorway, hands clenched at her sides. She was missing her two front teeth already, but one near the corner of her mouth hung loose, barely holding on. A thin string trailed from it, tied neatly to the doorknob.

Marilyn hovered just behind her, grinning wide, already covering her mouth like she couldn't believe they were really doing this.

"It's not gonna hurt," Marilyn said, though her voice cracked with laughter. "I promise."

On-screen, Alice squinted, suspicious.

"You said that last time," she said.

Thomas laughed. "That was a splinter."

The camera dipped as he adjusted his grip. Alice leaned closer to the television without realizing it, the wooden floor cool beneath her palms. She remembered this. The knot in her stomach. The way she'd felt brave and terrified at the same time.

"All right," Thomas said. "On three."

"One—"

Marilyn grabbed the doorknob.

"Two—"

The door swung shut.

The tooth came out clean.

No blood. No scream. Just a startled yelp that

turned into laughter as Alice stumbled back, clutching the string and the tiny white tooth dangling at the end.

"It's out!" Marilyn shouted. "Oh my God, it's out!"

On-screen, Alice beamed, eyes shining as she ran toward the camera, mouth open wide to show the gap. Thomas whooped, the sound bright and proud.

"That's my girl," he said.

Alice laughed softly along with them, warmth spreading through her chest. She remembered the way the air had smelled that day. Early fall. Leaves just starting to turn. The feeling that this—this small, stupid thing—was a milestone.

She reached for her wine and took a small sip, barely tasting it.

On the screen, she stopped in front of the camera, still grinning.

Her smile looked wrong.

Alice frowned.

It took her a second to see why.

The tooth was there.

Not fully seated. Not perfectly straight. But visible. Nestled back in place like it had never been pulled at all.

Her breath caught.

The tape didn't react.

No one said anything. Marilyn kept laughing behind her. Thomas praised her again, already turning the camera slightly, like the moment had passed.

The footage carried on for another few seconds, then cut to blue.

Alice stared at the screen.

Her pulse thudded in her ears, loud enough that it took a moment to notice the quiet hum of the VCR beneath it. She leaned back on her hands, grounding herself against the floor.

"That's...," she started, then stopped.

She reached forward and rewound the tape.

The machine whirred obediently, the sound mechanical and comforting. She waited until the footage rolled back far enough, then pressed play again.

The door.

The string.

"One—two—"

The tooth came out.

Alice ran toward the camera, smiling.

This time, the gap was there. Clean and unmistakable.

Her smile looked right.

Alice exhaled, the tension draining from her shoulders in a rush she hadn't realized she was holding. She let out a small, almost embarrassed laugh and shook her head.

"Bad angle," she murmured.

Or compression. Or the tape stretching. Or memory playing tricks on her.

The tape ended again, quietly.

Alice sat there for a moment longer, then pushed herself up and carried her empty wine glass into the kitchen. She rinsed it under the tap, the water loud in the still house, and set it upside down on the counter to dry. The simple motion helped. Grounded her.

When she came back, the living room felt unchanged. The plate still sat on the coffee table where she'd left it. The VCR waited patiently beneath the television.

She checked her phone without really thinking about it.

11:42

Alice blinked.

She lowered the phone, glanced at the dark window, then back at the screen. Late morning light still filled the room, slanting in at the same angle it had been before.

She shrugged it off.

"Guess I'm more tired than I thought," she said, mostly to hear her own voice.

Alice picked up the next tape and turned it over in her hands. She didn't check the date this time.

She slid it into the VCR and sat back down on the floor, closer than before.

The clock beneath the television glowed softly.

She pressed play.

The sound reached her before the image settled.

Her father's voice again—distant now, stretched thin, like it was coming through a wall. Laughter followed, but it didn't line up with what was on the screen. It arrived late, overlapping itself.

Alice blinked.

The picture wavered, then steadied. She relaxed despite herself, sinking back against the couch, the wooden floor cool beneath her legs. The wine sat warm and dull in her stomach. The room felt softer at the edges, less insistent.

She let her eyes close.

Just for a second.

The sound continued.

Footsteps on gravel. A door opening. Someone calling her name—drawn out, distorted, as if played at the wrong speed. Alice frowned in her sleep, brow tightening as the noise folded in on itself.

The laughter hollowed out.

Too slow.

Too close.

She dreamed of standing in a hallway again, smaller than she should have been, hands hanging uselessly at her sides. Voices drifted around her— happy voices—but the sound didn't match their movement. Words arrived before mouths opened. Laughter echoed before anything funny happened.

"Alice," someone said.

She turned—

And woke up.

The living room was dark.

Not dim.

Dark.

The television glowed faintly blue, its light barely reaching the walls. The VCR hummed beneath it, steady and patient. Alice sucked in a breath and pushed herself upright, heart pounding.

Her phone lay beside her on the floor.

She picked it up.

2:17

Her throat tightened.

She looked toward the window.

Outside, the yard was swallowed whole by shadow. The porch light was on. The street beyond was quiet, still, the kind of dark that had been there for a while.

Alice rubbed her face with both hands.

"Okay," she whispered. "Okay."

Her body felt heavy, stiff in a way that suggested more rest than she remembered taking. She stretched her legs and winced as sensation crept back in.

The house felt smaller now. Pressed in.

She sat back down and rewound the tape.

The machine clicked softly as it complied. Alice watched the screen, waiting for recognition. Waiting for the moment she remembered drifting off.

She pressed play.

The image was wrong.

Not the front door.

Not the yard.

Not her father's voice.

The camera faced a narrow hallway she didn't recognize at first. The walls were too close together, the ceiling lower than it should have been. A single light flickered overhead.

The footage moved forward slowly. Unsteadily.

Alice's stomach dropped.

This wasn't the tape she'd been watching.

She paused it. The frame froze mid-step, the edge of a door just visible ahead.

Her breath came shallow.

She rewound it again. Pressed play.

The hallway remained.

Different voices now. Not her parents'. Older. Flat. Someone talking off-camera about something mundane—keys, maybe. Or groceries. The sound didn't belong to the space it filled.

Alice shut the VCR off.

The room fell silent.

She sat there for a long moment, staring at her reflection in the dark screen, her face pale in the red glow of the clock beneath it.

She checked her phone again.

2:17

Outside, a car passed slowly down the street,

headlights sweeping briefly across the wall before fading away.

Alice swallowed.

"I must've grabbed the wrong tape," she said aloud, though the words felt thin as soon as she said them.

She picked up the case and turned it over in her hands.

It was the same one.

She didn't rewind it again.

Instead, Alice stood and went into the kitchen, rinsed her mouth at the sink, then leaned forward with both hands braced against the counter, breathing until her pulse slowed. The water tasted flat.

When she returned to the living room, the VCR clock still glowed beneath the television.

She didn't look at it.

Alice slid the tape back into its case and set it farther away than before. Then she reached for another—different scuffs, different weight—and carried it with her as she sat back down.

She pressed play.

The image wobbled as the camera adjusted. Grainy. Handheld. Too close to the floor at first, then lifting.

Marilyn's voice came through before she did, bright and amused.

"We caught your daddy working."

The camera swung toward the study. The door was already open. Inside, Thomas stood at the desk with his back half-turned, sleeves rolled up, a pencil paused mid-motion over a spread of papers. The desk was crowded—loose pages, notebooks, a calculator pushed aside like it had been forgotten. Equations filled the sheets in tight, deliberate lines.

He startled when they rushed in, then laughed—genuinely surprised, genuinely pleased. He lifted a hand to his face as he did, thumb brushing briefly beneath his nose, as if out of habit, before turning fully toward them.

Marilyn stepped closer, the camera drifting past the desk. A binder sat near the edge, thick and worn. Gray. Its corners frayed. A strip of duct tape was fixed to the top left, handwriting pressed hard into it:

PROPERTY OF THOMAS E. HOLLOWAY

Before the camera could settle, Thomas closed the binder without thinking. Not defensive. Just reflexive. Marilyn's focus lingered anyway, catching the printed text centered on the cover before drifting away.

ADAMS ASTROPHYSICS

Alice's voice piped up, breathless with excitement.

"Yeah, daddy is a scientist. I wanna be one just like him when I grow up."

She appeared at the edge of the frame then—

small, smiling, hands pressed to her stomach like she might burst from it all. Thomas turned fully toward her, his expression softening in a way Alice didn't remember often enough.

"Is that right?" he said. "You wanna be like your daddy?"

"Yes, daddy," Alice said, nodding hard.

Thomas smiled. He glanced at Marilyn, then back to Alice.

"And you're going to be that one day, huh?"

The tape clicked.

The image froze for a half second before cutting to black.

Alice frowned.

She rewound it.

The whirring sounded louder than it should have in the quiet room. She pressed play again.

The scene unfolded the same way. The laughter. The binder. The pride in his voice.

"And you're going to be that one day, huh?"

Alice sat back.

For a moment—longer than she expected—she could have sworn he'd said something else. Something sharper. Something that didn't belong there.

She told herself that was stupid.

She hadn't become a scientist. That was all. Life had gone a different way. She'd had Jesse young. She'd needed something steady. Something practical.

There was nothing wrong with that. She'd been good at it. She was good at it.

She finished the thought.

She stayed where she was.

The tape screen had gone dark, reflecting the room faintly back at her. Alice stared at it without really looking, her body still, her mind quiet in a way that didn't feel like relief.

She didn't notice how much time passed.

When the thought finally settled, nothing followed it. No movement. No decision. Just the continued act of sitting there, as if the moment required it.

As if standing up could wait.

❧ 4 ❧
REPETITION

It was her phone buzzing that startled her.

Not the sound itself, but how long it took her to recognize it.

The vibration came from the coffee table. Alice looked down at it, confused. Her phone lay face-up near the edge, the screen lighting the underside of the table in a dull, bluish glow. She could have sworn it had been in her pocket. She remembered the weight of it there. The outline against her thigh.

The buzzing stopped just as she reached for it.

The screen went dark.

Alice picked it up anyway, her thumb hovering where the answer button had been a second ago. No missed call. No voicemail notification. Nothing queued, nothing pending. The lock screen stared back at her like it always did.

She frowned.

It had been Jared. She was sure of it. The name had flashed there—briefly, but clearly enough that she didn't question it. He'd been checking in more lately. That made sense. Of course it was him.

She told herself it must have cut out early. Bad signal. A pocket dial that hadn't finished connecting. Something ordinary.

Alice lowered the phone to her lap and sat there for a moment longer than she needed to, waiting for it to buzz again.

It didn't.

She didn't check the time.

The television was already on.

Alice didn't remember turning it on, but she didn't question it either. The volume was low—just enough to fill the space without demanding her attention. Some daytime program she didn't recognize. A laugh track surfaced occasionally, out of place and brief, like it belonged to another room.

She moved past it toward the window.

The curtains were open.

Light spilled in across the living room floor, pale and flat, stretching farther than she expected. It felt later than it should have. She stood there for a moment, squinting, trying to reconcile the brightness with how tired she felt.

Without thinking, she reached out and pulled the curtains closed.

The room dimmed instantly. The television became more noticeable in the absence of light, its glow softening the edges of the furniture, rounding the corners of the space. Alice exhaled, the tension in her shoulders easing as if she'd corrected something that had been off.

She sat down.

The program continued. Voices rose and fell. A commercial break came and went. She watched none of it directly, but the sound anchored her there, a steady presence that made the quiet feel intentional instead of empty.

At some point, the room brightened again.

Alice looked up, startled, and realized the curtains were open.

She frowned, certain she'd just closed them. Certain enough that she checked the rod, the folds of fabric gathered neatly to either side. Sunlight filled the room again, warmer now. Later.

She stood and crossed the room, her movements automatic, and pulled the curtains shut once more.

The television flickered slightly as the light changed, then settled.

Alice returned to the couch.

She felt like she'd only just sat down.

The show had changed. Or maybe it hadn't. She couldn't tell. The voices blurred together now, familiar without being recognizable. Time seemed to compress around the sound, minutes slipping past without edges.

She blinked.

The room was brighter again.

Alice stared at the window, a slow confusion settling in—not alarm, not fear. Just a vague sense that something had skipped ahead without her permission.

She closed the curtains.

Again.

This time, she didn't sit down right away. She stood there, hand still resting on the fabric, listening to the television hum behind her. The house felt calm. Maintained. As if this was what it was meant to feel like.

When she finally sat, the light outside was already changing.

She didn't notice.

Her mouth felt dry.

Alice noticed it only after she swallowed and nothing happened—no relief, no change. Just the sensation staying where it was. She pressed her tongue to the roof of her mouth, frowning slightly, then stood and went to the kitchen.

She didn't remember deciding to.

The overhead light felt too bright. She squinted and opened the fridge, staring into it longer than necessary. There was food there. Enough of it. Things she could heat up, things that required more effort than she wanted to think about.

She closed the fridge.

The dryness lingered. She opened a cabinet instead, then another. Glasses lined the shelf exactly where they always were. She reached for one, then stopped.

Her eyes drifted to the counter.

The bottle of Cabernet was already there.

She couldn't remember taking it out, but the cork was halfway off, tilted at an angle that suggested it had been opened recently. Not fresh. Just... open enough.

Alice hesitated, then shrugged.

She poured without measuring, the dark liquid filling the glass more than she intended. The smell rose immediately—familiar, grounding. She took a sip.

It helped. A little.

The dryness eased, though it didn't disappear completely. She took another sip, slower this time, and leaned back against the counter. Only then did she realize how hollow her stomach felt—not sharp hunger, not pain. Just an absence she hadn't noticed building.

She thought about eating.

The thought finished neatly, like it always did.

She stayed where she was.

The television murmured from the other room, steady and unconcerned. Alice took another sip and set the glass down, meaning to move in a second. Just long enough to decide what to make.

She stood there longer than that.

By the time she returned to the living room, the light had shifted again. The curtains were open. The TV had changed programs. The glass in her hand was nearly empty.

Alice sat down and reached for the remote.

She didn't remember bringing the wine with her.

After the hallway was empty, Alice didn't get up again.

She lay there with her eyes closed, the television murmuring softly behind her eyelids. Her breathing slowed on its own. The dryness in her mouth faded. The tightness in her chest loosened, leaving behind a dull, manageable calm.

Whatever that had been—dream, shadow, trick of the light—it was gone now. The house felt settled again. Familiar. Quiet in the way it always had been.

She slept.

This time, deeply.

No half-waking.

No interruption.

No sense of time passing strangely.

When she shifted against the couch, it was

without thought, her body finding a comfortable position and staying there. The television eventually went to static, then silence. Night moved across the windows without her noticing.

Alice rested in a way she hadn't in days.

And when she woke later, she would remember this sleep as the last good one.

5

LAG

A lice woke up thirsty.

The sensation arrived first, fully formed, before she understood what it was asking for. Her mouth felt thick and dry, the kind of dryness that lingered even after she swallowed. She lay still for a moment, eyes closed, waiting for the feeling to pass the way it usually did.

It didn't.

When she opened her eyes, the room felt wrong

in a way she couldn't place. Not darker. Not unfamiliar. Just... behind. Like her body had woken up before the space around it had caught up.

The television was off.

That took her a second to register. She was sure she'd fallen asleep with it on. She remembered the sound, the low murmur filling the room as she drifted under. Now the silence pressed in gently, without urgency.

Alice sat up.

Her head lagged behind the motion, a dull pressure blooming at her temples before settling again. She waited for the discomfort to resolve before standing.

It took longer than she expected.

She swung her legs over the side of the couch and stood, steadying herself with the armrest. The thirst remained. Stronger now. She headed toward the kitchen, each step feeling slightly delayed—like the intention had been issued earlier and was only just being carried out.

Sunlight filtered in through the window.

Alice squinted. It felt too bright for morning. Or maybe not bright enough for afternoon. She couldn't tell. The thought slipped away before it finished forming.

She filled a glass with water and drank half of it in one go. The relief came late, dull and incomplete, like an echo of what it should have been. She drank the rest more slowly, waiting for her body to catch up.

It didn't.

She stood there, glass empty in her hand, aware of the moment stretching longer than it needed to. The kitchen clock ticked softly behind her.

Alice didn't turn to look at it.

Instead, she set the glass down and leaned against the counter, telling herself she'd move in a second. Just long enough for the feeling to pass.

It would.

Eventually.

Alice stayed in the kitchen longer than she meant to.

She stood near the counter, hands resting against its edge, waiting for the feeling to pass the way these things usually did. It didn't sharpen. It didn't fade. It just lingered—dull, persistent, like pressure behind the eyes.

The television murmured from the other room.

She turned toward the sound without thinking, drawn by it the way she had been all day. The living room light was softer, more forgiving. Familiar. She crossed the threshold and sat down where she always did, letting her body settle before her thoughts caught up.

The cushions dipped beneath her weight. The room felt quieter here. Contained.

Alice leaned back and fixed her eyes on the television, not really watching it, just letting the movement and sound carry her forward. Her breathing slowed. The tension in her shoulders loosened a fraction.

She told herself she'd rest for a minute.

She was sitting in the living room.

The television murmured softly, the light from it washing over the walls the same way it always had. Alice felt herself drifting—not asleep, not fully awake. Just loosening. Her thoughts slipped backward without resistance, settling somewhere older.

She was nine.

The house was the same, but smaller. Or maybe she was. The living room felt louder then, fuller somehow. She sat in the same place she was sitting now, feet tucked beneath her, listening.

Voices rose upstairs.

Not words at first—just tone. Sharp. Uneven. The sound of something breaking apart without fully falling.

Alice stood.

In the dream, she didn't question it. She moved toward the stairs and climbed them, each step familiar, worn into her memory. The voices grew clearer as she reached the top. Her parents' bedroom door was cracked open.

She slowed.

The light inside the room was on. Too bright.

She crept closer and peeked through the opening.

Her mother stood near the bed, a wine glass clenched in one hand, the liquid inside sloshing dangerously close to the rim. Marilyn's face was flushed, her movements sharp and unsteady.

"You baby her," Marilyn shouted. "You always have. You don't even see it."

Thomas stood near the edge of the bed, hands open at his sides like he was trying not to startle her. "I don't," he said, his voice tight but controlled. "I don't baby her."

Marilyn laughed—a short, ugly sound—and stepped closer. "You do," she said. "Every time she looks at you, you cave."

Before Alice could process what was happening, Marilyn's hand came up and struck Thomas across the face.

The sound cracked through the room.

Alice burst forward, the door swinging open as she screamed, "Stop!"

Marilyn turned on her instantly, pointing toward the hallway with the hand that wasn't holding the glass. "Get out," she screamed. "Get out!"

"She doesn't need to!" Thomas said, his voice breaking through the room like a line drawn in chalk.

Marilyn snapped back toward him, eyes wild. "There you go," she shouted. "Doing it again!"

Then she was gone—storming past Alice, down the stairs, her footsteps heavy and uneven. A moment later, something clinked loudly in the kitchen below.

The room fell silent.

Thomas sat down on the bed slowly, like his legs had given up on him. He stared at the floor, his shoulders sagging. When he spoke, it wasn't to Alice. It was to himself.

"She used to not be like this," he whispered. "I don't know how or why..."

His face crumpled. He covered it with his hands and began to cry.

Alice stepped toward him.

She reached up, placing her small hands on either side of his face, forcing him to look at her. "It's okay, daddy," she said. "I love you. I'll never be mean to you."

—

Alice woke with a sharp breath.

She was back on the couch.

Her hands were raised in front of her, fingers curved exactly as they had been in the dream, as if she were still holding her father's face. She lowered them slowly, her heart racing.

The room felt wrong.

Not unfamiliar—but charged. Like the air itself remembered something she didn't. The emotion lingered, thick and unresolved, pressing in on her chest.

Alice sat there, shaken, unable to tell how long she'd been gone.

The feeling didn't leave.

Alice remained seated for a while longer.

She wasn't sure what she was waiting for—only that standing still felt wrong, and moving felt delayed, like the signal hadn't quite reached her yet. The room held the memory of the dream too well. The air felt charged, unfinished.

She lowered her hands to her lap and stared at them, flexing her fingers once, then again. The movement felt faintly disconnected, as if she were watching herself do it from half a step behind.

The television murmured.

She hadn't turned it back on.

Alice frowned, lifting her head. The screen glowed softly now, picture indistinct, sound low enough that it blended with the house's quiet instead of breaking it. She reached for the remote and pressed the power button.

Nothing happened.

She pressed it again.

The screen went dark a full second later—long enough that she wondered if it hadn't worked at all.

Her chest tightened.

"Okay," she murmured, not annoyed so much as tired.

She stood, the room tilting just slightly after the fact, and waited for it to settle. When it did, she moved toward the hallway.

The house felt... behind her.

Not resisting. Just slow to update.

At the base of the stairs, she paused. The light above was on, spilling faintly into the hall, warmer than it should have been for the hour she thought it was. She rested her hand on the banister, grounding herself in the familiar groove worn into the wood.

Her parents' bedroom sat at the end of the hall upstairs.

She didn't look at it directly.

Instead, her gaze shifted to the study door below —half visible from where she stood, the corner of it catching the light. The room felt heavier than the others. Contained. Like something had been waiting there longer than she had.

Alice turned toward it.

As she walked, the sensation returned—that slight delay, like her body had decided before her thoughts caught up. She reached the study door and pushed it open.

The hinges didn't creak.

That struck her as wrong immediately.

Inside, the room smelled faintly of dust and old paper. The shelves lined the walls just as she remembered—binders, books, folders stacked with quiet intent. The desk sat beneath the window, un-touched.

Alice stepped inside.

The overhead light flicked on a moment after her hand left the switch.

She froze, then exhaled slowly.

"Get a grip," she said, not unkindly.

Her eyes moved across the shelves. Newspaper clippings lay stacked in uneven piles—some yellowed, some crisp, their headlines too small to read from where she stood. She felt a pull toward them, a sense that they mattered, though she couldn't have said why.

On the desk, partially hidden beneath a folder, sat a familiar shape.

A binder.

Gray. Worn. Its corners frayed from use.

Alice's breath slowed.

She reached for it—and stopped.

The hesitation wasn't fear. It was something closer to anticipation, mixed with the strange certainty that once she opened it, something would shift. Not resolve. Just... move.

Her fingers brushed the edge.

The room seemed to hold still around her, waiting for the action to finish catching up.

Alice didn't open the binder yet.

She closed her eyes instead, steadying herself,

aware of the way her heart had begun to beat just a little faster—not panic, not distress.

Focus.

When she opened her eyes again, the decision felt already made.

And for the first time since returning to the house, Alice understood the feeling clearly:

She wasn't remembering by accident anymore.

She was starting to look.

Alice lifted one of the clippings from the pile.

She hadn't meant to read it—only to move it aside—but her eyes caught on a name halfway down the column. She paused, then drew the paper closer.

Dr. Arthur Adams, it read.

The article itself was dry. Measured. A few quoted lines about signal data and observation. Words chosen carefully enough to say nothing at all. She skimmed once, then again, slower this time.

Her gaze drifted back to the desk.

The binder sat where she had left it. Gray. Worn. Familiar in the way old work was familiar—handled often, but never fondly. She hadn't touched it, but now she noticed the stamp at the center of the cover.

ADAMS ASTROPHYSICS

Alice felt the click before she understood it.

Not a realization. A connection.

She looked from the name on the page to the

logo on the binder, then back again, as if expecting one of them to change. They didn't.

Her pulse picked up, light and quick, the way it did when something started to line up. Not fear. Not dread.

Focus.

She set the clipping down beside the binder, careful to align their edges. The sameness between them felt louder than any explanation could have been.

"Okay," she whispered.

The word didn't calm her.

It steadied her.

She reached for the binder.

Alice didn't remember deciding to go into the study.

She was standing in the doorway one moment, and inside it the next, the room dimmer than the rest of the house, the air heavier — not stale, just held. Like it didn't like being disturbed.

The desk sat exactly where it always had.

She moved toward it slowly, her shoulder twinging faintly as she leaned down and opened the lower drawer. Inside were old folders, notebooks, loose papers that smelled faintly of dust and ink.

The binder was still there.

Gray. Worn. Duct tape at the corner.

She lifted it out carefully, as if it might resist.

The cover bent slightly as she opened it — not

stiff with neglect, but softened with use. The first thing inside wasn't paper.

It was a photograph.

Alice's breath caught.

Her father stood in the frame, younger than she remembered him, smiling openly at the camera. She sat on his shoulders, barely more than a baby, her small hands tangled in his hair. They were at the park near the house — she recognized the tree behind them instantly.

She touched the edge of the photo with her thumb.

Someone had taken this.

The realization arrived quietly, without ceremony.

Marilyn.

For a moment, Alice just sat there, the binder open in her lap, the image blurring as her eyes burned. This wasn't a memory she carried. It was proof that something good had existed — that she hadn't imagined it.

She slid the photo back into place.

Beneath it were papers. Typed notes. Handwritten margins. Diagrams she didn't recognize.

She didn't read closely. Not yet.

"...three-day saturation window..."

"...disappearances..."

"...neural output remains consistent once ATP production stabilizes..."

. . .

She frowned, the words slipping through her grasp as soon as she tried to hold onto them. They didn't settle. They didn't connect.

At the bottom of the page, printed cleanly beneath a header, was a name she'd seen before.

Dr. Arthur Adams

Adams Astrophysics

Alice stared at it longer than necessary.

The same name she'd half-heard on the television.

The same name that had flickered past without staying.

She closed the binder.

Not because she was done — but because she wasn't ready.

The house didn't react.

It didn't need to.

6

IDLE

A lice woke up already tired.

Not the kind of tired that came from poor sleep, or grief, or crying herself out the night before. This was different—flat, persistent. Like her body had been left running too long without going anywhere.

She lay still on the couch, eyes open, watching the ceiling fan rotate lazily above her. It wasn't on.

She knew that. But the blades looked like they were moving anyway, just barely, as if the air itself hadn't finished deciding what it was doing.

Her mouth was dry again.

She swallowed once. Then again. The sensation didn't go away.

Alice sat up slowly. The room lagged behind her movement—just enough that she noticed it. The couch dipped. The blanket slid to the floor. Somewhere in the house, a pipe ticked softly as it cooled.

Everything worked.

Nothing felt urgent.

She checked her phone.

No new notifications.

The time made sense. She didn't linger on it. She'd learned better than that.

Alice stood and went to the kitchen, filling a glass with water and drinking it down in long, steady gulps. She waited for relief.

It came late. Dull. Incomplete.

She stood there longer than necessary, glass still in her hand, staring at the counter as if she were waiting for instructions that never arrived.

Eventually, she set the glass down.

The television turned on behind her.

Alice didn't flinch this time. She didn't even turn around right away. The sound filled the house—low, conversational, inoffensive. Daytime voices discussing something that didn't matter.

She exhaled.

"Okay," she murmured.

When she returned to the living room, the program was already halfway through. She sat down without adjusting the cushions, without checking the remote. The light through the window was steady. The curtains were open.

She left them that way.

Minutes passed. Or longer. The show ended. Another began. Alice watched without watching, her thoughts slipping into neutral grooves—chores she could do later, food she might eat, nothing sharp enough to hurt.

Her body felt... manageable.

That was new.

No spikes.

No drops.

Just a smooth, even hum.

Alice leaned her head back and closed her eyes.

For a moment—just one—she had the distinct, unshakable sense that something was continuing without her.

Not moving forward.

Not ending.

Just... running.

She opened her eyes again.

The feeling was gone.

The television kept talking.

Alice stayed where she was.

Her phone began to ring.

Alice didn't move right away. The sound layered itself over the television, sharp but not urgent. She reached for the phone after a moment, answering without checking the screen.

"Hello?"

There was nothing on the other end.

No voice.

No static.

No sound at all.

She listened, eyes still open, gaze unfocused on the far wall.

"Hello?" she said again.

The call ended.

Alice pulled the phone away from her ear. The screen had already gone dark. No missed call. No active call. No indication it had happened.

She set the phone back down on the cushion beside her.

The television kept talking.

Alice stayed where she was.

The television continued on its own. A voice rose, another answered. Laughter surfaced and faded without pulling her in.

After a while, she stood.

The bathroom light came on too bright, then settled. She turned the shower handle and waited.

The water took a moment to register—warmth arriving late, spreading unevenly. Alice stepped under it and closed her eyes.

She stood there longer than necessary. Steam gathered, softened the edges of the room. The water ran over her shoulders and down her back. It caught briefly along the pale scar on her left shoulder before continuing on, the sensation thinning as it moved past it.

She didn't linger on it.

Eventually, she turned the water off because there was nothing else to do.

She dried off slowly. Her towel slipped once and she adjusted it without urgency. Her body felt present in pieces, like sensation had been distributed unevenly and never fully reassembled.

Hunger arrived sometime later. Not sharp. Not demanding. Just there.

Alice went into the kitchen and made something simple. She didn't remember deciding what to eat. Her hands moved anyway. While it warmed, she poured a glass of wine and took a sip without tasting it, then set it down where she could forget about it.

Her phone began to ring.

Alice stood still, listening to it. The sound filled the kitchen briefly, then stopped between rings. She reached for the phone a moment too late.

The screen was dark.

No missed call. No notification. Nothing to respond to.

She set the phone back down and returned to what she had been doing.

The television was still on when she brought the food back to the couch. She didn't change the channel. She sat and ate while it talked.

The food was hot, but the flavor didn't land. Texture came through more clearly than taste. She chewed, swallowed, took another bite. It wasn't bad. It just didn't register the way she expected it to. She added salt without thinking. It didn't help.

The show shifted into something else at some point. She watched a scene end without remembering how it began.

Her fork slowed. She took the last bite, set it down, and leaned back.

That was when she remembered the VCR.

The small red light was on—steady, unobtrusive —like it had been that way for a while.

Alice stayed where she was.

7

PERSISTENCE

A lice noticed the light before she noticed the reason she was still sitting there.

The television had gone quiet again—not off, just between things. The room felt thinner without it. The silence didn't bother her so much as the absence of something to hold onto. She stared at the darkened screen, then let her eyes drift lower.

The red glow beneath it was steady.

The VCR.

She didn't remember when she'd first seen it. It felt like it had always been there, tucked beneath the television like an afterthought. The light hadn't drawn her attention before. It didn't blink or pulse.

It simply stayed on, patient, as if waiting for her to notice.

Alice shifted forward on the couch. Her joints protested faintly, delayed, like everything else lately. She stood and remained standing for a second longer than necessary, the room catching up around her.

"I just want something else on," she murmured.

Not the news. Not voices talking past her. Something quieter. Something older. Something that didn't expect anything from her.

She turned toward the hallway.

The study door was open.

She paused there, hand resting on the frame, listening. The house didn't react. It never did. She stepped inside.

The study felt cooler than the rest of the house, not draft-cold—contained. The shelves were lined with binders and boxes she hadn't looked through yet. Against the back wall, half-hidden behind a chair, sat the small shelving unit.

The tapes were still there.

Alice crouched and ran her fingers along the spines without reading them, stopping at random. The cases were worn, softened at the edges from handling. She pulled one free.

The label was handwritten. Faded. Familiar in a way she couldn't place.

She didn't think about it long enough to second-guess herself.

Back in the living room, she slid the tape into the VCR. The machine accepted it immediately, the soft mechanical click sounding louder than it should have. The screen flickered once, then filled with static before resolving into color.

A timestamp appeared in the corner.

Alice lowered herself onto the floor without realizing she'd meant to, sitting close to the television, legs folded beneath her. The room behind her felt distant now. Secondary.

The tape began.

The image was unsteady.

For a moment, all Alice could see was fabric—dark, close, moving. The camera tilted, then settled. A narrow space came into view. Shelves lined with clothes. Shoes scattered on the floor. A closet.

Her mother sat on the floor with her back against the wall.

Marilyn's hair was loose, strands clinging to her face. A wine bottle rested on its side near her knee, red spreading across the carpet in a dark, uneven bloom. The smell seemed to reach Alice through the screen, sharp and familiar.

Marilyn laughed suddenly, the sound breaking apart halfway through.

"Oh," she said, pressing the heel of her hand into her eye. "Oh, Alice. I didn't mean for you to see me like this."

Alice—the Alice in the recording—stood just

inside the doorway. The camera angle hovered low, uncertain, as if whoever was holding it hadn't meant to be.

"I was screaming, wasn't I?" Marilyn continued, wiping her face with the back of her sleeve. "That's probably what did it. I'm sorry, sweetheart. I really am."

She gestured vaguely toward the floor, the bottle, herself.

"This isn't... this isn't me at my best."

She took a breath that hitched on the way in.

"You know your dad?" Marilyn asked. She smiled faintly, the expression fragile, like it might fold in on itself. "God, he's an amazing man. He really is. He sees the best in people. In everyone. Even when they don't deserve it."

Her voice wavered, then steadied again.

"My dad," she said, quieter now, "he ruined men for me. Gave me a bad taste I didn't even know I had. I thought that was just how it was. How it always felt."

She shook her head slowly.

"And then I met Thomas. And it felt like I could finally breathe."

Marilyn laughed again, softer this time, and leaned her head back against the wall.

"I wasn't very good at that," she admitted. "Breathing."

She looked directly toward the camera then. Toward Alice.

"I'm embarrassed," she said. "And I'm hurt. And I hate that you're seeing this. You shouldn't have to."

Her eyes shone, unfocused but intent.

"I'm going to do better," Marilyn said. "I want to do better. I promise."

The word hung there, too heavy for the small space.

The camera shifted slightly, as if the person holding it didn't know where to look anymore.

Marilyn reached out, stopping herself halfway, then let her hand fall back to her side.

"I love you," she said. "I really do."

The image shook. The sound cut briefly, then returned.

The tape ended.

The screen went blue.

Alice didn't move.

Her chest felt tight—not sharp, not painful. Just full. Like something had been placed there without her permission and left behind. She pressed her palm flat against the floor, grounding herself in the cool wood.

The VCR hummed softly beneath the television.

Alice stared at the blank screen, the promise echoing louder now than it had any right to.

She didn't stop the tape.

Instead she rewound it.

The VCR answered immediately, the low mechanical whir filling the space beneath the television. The blue screen dissolved into static as the image slid backward, color and motion collapsing in on themselves.

She pressed play.

The hum stopped.

The picture returned.

A front door filled the frame.

The camera sat low, angled slightly upward, as if it had been set down without intention. Two uniformed figures stood on the porch, shifting their weight as they waited. One of them raised a hand and knocked.

The sound landed heavier than it should have.

Footsteps approached from inside. The door opened.

Thomas stood there.

He looked tired—not disheveled, not unwell. Just worn thin, like something had already been pulling at him long before this moment arrived.

"Yes?" he said.

The officers spoke calmly. Their voices were even, practiced. The words themselves seemed ordinary until they finished saying them.

There had been an accident.

Marilyn had been involved.

They were sorry.

Thomas didn't respond right away. His expression held, fixed in place, but his body shifted. He reached out suddenly and gripped one of the officer's shoulders, fingers tightening as if the ground beneath him had tilted.

"I'm sorry," the officer said again, quieter this time.

Thomas nodded once.

Then his knees gave out.

The camera dipped as whoever was holding it reacted too late. The frame caught Thomas folding inward, the sound of him hitting the floor dull and final.

Alice moved into view.

She was smaller here. Twelve. Her movements were uncertain but immediate, her hesitation lasting only a fraction of a second before she knelt beside him.

"Dad?" she said.

Thomas's eyes were open, unfocused. He stared past her, breathing shallowly, as if the air itself had thickened around him.

The officers knelt too, voices lowered now, asking questions that didn't seem to expect answers. Was there someone they could call. Family. A neighbor.

Thomas shook his head faintly.

"I'm okay," he said, though the words barely carried.

Alice leaned closer, pressing her shoulder against

his arm, staying there because she didn't know what else to do.

The camera wavered, then steadied.

There was no timestamp in the corner.

The image held longer than it needed to—Thomas on the floor, Alice beside him, the officers waiting for something to happen that didn't.

Then the picture flickered.

Not to blue. Just a brief wash of static.

The tape kept going.

The static cleared on its own.

The image sharpened without warning.

The camera was moving now. Not smoothly—carried, jostled slightly, the way something is when no one is paying attention to how they're holding it. The world tilted and righted itself in small, uncertain increments.

Alice's hand rose to her mouth.

She didn't realize she'd done it until her fingers touched her lips. She stayed like that, palm pressed lightly against her face, eyes fixed on the screen.

The camera passed through a doorway. Light flared briefly, then dimmed.

A church.

Wooden pews filled the frame, their backs worn smooth by use. People sat in rows, some leaning toward one another, others staring straight ahead. The camera drifted, unanchored, as if searching for where it was supposed to be.

A timestamp appeared in the corner.

Alice's gaze flicked to it for half a second, then back to the center of the screen.

At the front of the room, a casket rested beneath soft, too-warm lighting. Flowers crowded around it, overwhelming, excessive. The lid was closed.

Voices murmured. Coughed. Shifted.

The camera settled into a seat.

Thomas sat near the aisle. He looked smaller here somehow, folded inward, his hands clasped together so tightly his knuckles had gone pale. He didn't look at the casket. He didn't look anywhere in particular.

Someone touched his shoulder. He nodded without turning.

The service began.

Words filled the space—measured, practiced, meant to comfort. They passed over the camera without landing. The lens drifted occasionally, catching fragments: a bowed head, a folded program, someone wiping their eyes too late.

Alice watched herself in the frame only once.

She sat beside Thomas, feet not quite reaching the floor, hands folded in her lap exactly the way she'd been told to. Her face was still. Too still. She didn't cry. She didn't frown. She watched the front of the room as if she were waiting for something to happen.

Nothing did.

The timestamp remained.

The camera never zoomed in.

The service ended the way these things always did—chairs scraping softly, people standing, voices lowering into careful tones. Someone said they were sorry. Someone else said she was in a better place.

The words stacked up without meaning.

The image followed Thomas and Alice down the aisle. The light outside flared again, brighter than before, washing the edges of the frame.

Alice on the floor didn't move.

Her hand stayed at her mouth. Her breathing was shallow but steady. She didn't reach for the remote. She didn't look away.

The tape ended and the screen went blue.

The blue screen lingered.

The VCR hummed softly beneath the television, steady and unbothered.

Alice reached forward and pressed eject.

The machine clicked, and the tape slid partway out, warm to the touch when she pulled it free. She didn't look at the label this time. She didn't rewind it again.

She set it aside on the floor, a little farther away than the others.

For a moment, she stayed where she was, knees drawn in, the television filling the room with its low, empty glow. The silence felt different now. Thicker. Like something had been left open.

Alice stood and turned back toward the hallway.

The study was still open.

She walked there slowly, the house lagging behind her steps the way it had been all day. The shelves waited exactly where she remembered them. The small shelving unit sat against the wall, unchanged.

She reached out and pulled another tape free.

This one felt heavier.

She didn't know why.

Back in the living room, she slid it into the VCR. The machine accepted it immediately, the soft mechanical sound familiar now—expected.

The screen flickered.

The tape began.

The image wavered, then steadied.

The camera faced the doorway of the study, angled slightly downward, as if it had been set on a shelf or propped against something nearby. The room beyond was quiet. Too still.

Thomas sat at his desk.

He hadn't moved.

His shoulders were slightly hunched, his hands resting flat on either side of an open binder. The pages lay exposed beneath the desk lamp, filled with tight lines of writing and diagrams that didn't seem to matter to him anymore. His gaze was fixed on the paper, unfocused—looking through it rather than at it.

"A little too still," Alice murmured under her breath, without realizing she had.

On the tape, a younger Alice appeared in the doorway. Twelve. Thinner than she remembered being. Her hair hung loose around her shoulders, unbrushed.

"Dad," she said.

No response.

She took a step inside.

"Dad?"

Still nothing.

She raised her voice slightly, more urgency than fear.

"Dad!"

Thomas jolted.

His shoulders snapped upright as if pulled by a string. One hand twitched against the desk, knocking a pen to the floor. He blinked rapidly, eyes struggling to focus as he turned toward the doorway.

"Oh—" He exhaled sharply, then softened immediately. "Sorry, sweetie. I was... I was deep in thought."

Alice stood there for a moment, her hands clasped loosely in front of her. She didn't say anything right away.

Thomas shifted in his chair, clearing his throat. "What do you need?"

She shook her head. "Nothing. I just wanted to check in on you."

He smiled faintly. It didn't reach his eyes, but the effort was there.

"I'm fine," he said quickly. Too quickly. "Really."

She hesitated, then took another step closer. "You know you can talk to me," she said. "I love you."

Something flickered across his face—surprise, then something heavier beneath it. He pushed back from the desk just enough to lean forward and kissed her on the forehead.

"I love you too," he said.

He stayed seated.

Alice turned and walked out of the study. The camera didn't follow her. It remained fixed on Thomas as she reached back and pulled the door closed behind her.

Not all the way.

The latch didn't click.

For a few seconds, nothing happened.

Thomas stared at the binder again. His jaw tightened. His hands curled slowly into fists against the edge of the desk.

Then his face folded.

He brought one hand up to his mouth as a sound escaped him—quiet at first, like a breath gone wrong. His shoulders began to shake. He leaned forward, elbows braced on the desk, and pressed his forehead into his palm as the sobs broke through fully.

He cried without sound for a moment.

Then the sound came.

Raw. Uncontrolled. The kind of crying that doesn't ask to be heard.

The camera continued to record.

The image didn't cut.

It didn't stop.

Instead, the sound softened gradually, bleeding into a low, ambient hiss as the picture dimmed—not to blue, not to black, but to something in between.

The tape kept playing.

The image shifted without warning.

The study was brighter now. Or darker. Alice couldn't tell which came first.

Thomas sat in the same chair, at the same desk. The binder was still open, but a different page lay exposed. Or maybe the same one. The desk lamp hummed faintly, the sound just loud enough to notice when nothing else was moving.

Alice stood beside him.

"Dad?" she said.

He didn't answer right away.

She waited, hands clasped behind her back, eyes moving across the room in small, careful sweeps. The shelves. The window. The carpet beneath her feet.

"Dad."

Thomas blinked.

"Oh—sorry," he said, turning his head toward her a fraction too late. "What is it, sweetie?"

"I was just checking on you," she said. "Did you eat?"

He looked down at the binder, then back up again. "I will in a minute."

She nodded, though that hadn't been what she asked.

A beat passed.

"Do you want me to make you something?" she tried.

Thomas picked up his pen. Set it back down. "I just need to finish this first."

Alice glanced at the page. It was filled edge to edge with writing, tight and deliberate. She didn't recognize any of it.

She waited for him to look at her.

He didn't.

The image jumped again.

The light outside the window had shifted. Late afternoon now, casting long lines across the floor. Thomas hadn't moved from the chair. The binder lay open in the same position, the corners of the pages slightly curled.

Alice stood closer this time, a glass of water in her hands.

"I brought you this," she said.

Thomas didn't react until she set it down beside him.

"Thank you," he said, gently. Automatically.

She watched his face as he spoke, searching for something she couldn't name. He smiled at her—soft, reassuring—but his eyes didn't quite land.

"You're doing great," he added, as if responding to a thought she hadn't voiced.

Her throat tightened.

"I miss Mom," Alice said quietly.

Thomas nodded. "I know."

The answer came too fast. Too smooth.

"She'd be proud of you," he continued. "You're a good girl."

Alice didn't move.

That wasn't what she'd meant.

The image shifted again.

The room was dim now. The desk lamp cast a small circle of light, leaving the corners in shadow. Thomas rubbed his face with both hands, dragging his palms down slowly as if trying to wake himself up.

"Okay," he muttered.

He flipped a page in the binder. Then flipped it back.

"Okay," he said again, louder this time. His jaw tightened. "Just—okay."

Alice hovered near the doorway, half in, half out of the frame. She watched him the way someone watches a stove they're afraid to touch.

"Dad?" she said.

He startled, shoulders jerking.

"I'm fine," he snapped—then immediately softened. "Sorry. I didn't mean that. I'm just... tired."

He reached for the glass of water. Missed it. Tried again. His hand closed around it on the second attempt.

"I'm fine," he repeated, quieter now. "Don't worry about me."

He didn't drink.

The image jumped.

Thomas sat slumped forward, elbows on the desk, one hand tangled in his hair. The binder was closed now, pushed slightly to the side. A bottle sat where the glass of water had been.

Alice stood just outside the room.

Thomas laughed suddenly—a short, humorless sound that startled even him.

"Can't... can't keep doing this," he said, shaking his head. "Just—just need it to slow down."

He lifted the bottle and drank without reacting, his gaze unfixed, drifting somewhere beyond the desk.

Alice took a step forward.

"Dad?"

He didn't answer.

He took another drink.

"I know," he said, to no one. "I know. I'm trying."

His voice shifted, anger flickering through it like a bad signal. "Just give me a second."

Then concern, immediately after. "You shouldn't be seeing this."

Then sadness, heavy and unguarded. "I didn't mean for it to be like this."

The cycle didn't resolve.

It reset.

The camera kept recording.

Alice didn't remember reaching for the bottle.

She noticed it only when it was already in her hand, the glass cool against her palm. She took a swallow without looking at the screen, the taste dull and familiar, then another. The room stayed steady. The television murmured on.

The image shifted.

Alice looked up.

The hallway came into view—upstairs. Narrower than she remembered it. The camera sat low and slightly off-center, like it had been set down without care and left there. Daylight filtered in from the window at the far end of the hall, pale and ordinary, cutting across the floor in a clean strip.

From the far end, a voice carried.

Thomas.

He stood just outside the parents' bedroom, one shoulder resting against the doorframe. The door behind him was open, the room beyond dim but intact. A bottle rested on the dresser inside, catching a thin band of late-morning light.

He looked unwell.

Not frantic. Not panicked. Just worn down—his face slack with a kind of exhaustion that sleep wouldn't touch. His eyes were open, unfocused.

Aimed down the hall.

Toward Alice's room.

The younger Alice stood behind her closed door. The image shifted slightly as she cracked it open, careful, hesitant.

"Dad?" she said.

He didn't answer her.

Instead, he spoke softly, almost conversationally.

"You've been here all along."

He wasn't angry.

He wasn't afraid.

He sounded finished.

Alice pushed her door open a little more. Her shoulder slipped past the frame, bare to the hallway. She leaned forward, trying to see his face more clearly. Trying to understand who he was speaking to.

The air changed.

Not with sound.

Not with movement.

With presence.

Something occupied the space between them.

Not advancing. Not reaching. Just there—filling the hallway the way pressure fills a sealed room.

Light still came from the window. Late-morning light. Ordinary light. It moved as it should—until it reached the space between Alice and her father.

There, it thinned.

Not dimmed.

Thinned—bending around something that did not reflect it, did not interrupt it, but reduced the room it had to exist in.

The hallway darkened only by subtraction.

For a moment, the world felt slightly muted—

not gone, not silent,

just turned down enough that nothing pushed back.

Then sound stopped belonging to the space.

The house didn't go silent.

Instead, everything audible seemed suddenly too far away—as if the distance between Alice and the world had stretched without warning. Her breath still moved in her chest, but she couldn't hear it. The hum of the house persisted somewhere beyond reach, detached from proximity.

Thomas didn't move.

The pressure increased.

Not as force.

As completion.

Alice was thrown backward.

Her shoulder struck the doorframe hard enough

to knock the air from her lungs. Sensation arrived late—blunted, distant—like it had taken too long to find her.

The image cut.

The screen went black.

The tape kept running.

For a moment, nothing appeared—just darkness, faint static at the edges.

Then a timestamp blinked into the corner of the screen.

11:42

It didn't flicker.

It didn't count.

It simply stayed.

8

SATURATION

Alice didn't move when the screen went black. The tape had ended, but the corner of the image still held something—an after-image that didn't belong to the room. A timestamp sitting there like it had been burned into the glass. The television's glow flattened the living room into shapes: couch, coffee table, the dark mouth of the hallway.

Alice stayed on the floor.

Her throat felt too tight to swallow, and her body didn't know what to do with that, so it chose something else.

Her hand reached for the wine bottle without consulting her brain.

The glass was cool against her palm. Familiar. She lifted it to her mouth and tipped it back.

Nothing came out.

Not a drip. Not a slow pour. Just air—and the brief humiliation of expecting comfort from something that couldn't even pretend anymore.

She stared at the bottle, tipped it again like that would change the truth. Still nothing. Empty.

A small laugh tried to leave her chest and failed halfway out.

"Okay," she whispered.

She didn't sound scared. She sounded... finished. Like Thomas had.

The bottle slipped from her hand and thudded onto the floor beside the couch. It didn't break. It just rolled an inch and stopped, as if it had found its place.

Alice sat there for another second, staring at the dead screen, and then her fingers went to her purse —fast, automatic, like her hand had memorized the route.

Receipts. Keys. Jesse's funeral program, soft at the folds.

And then:

Metal.

Her flask.

She didn't pause to feel ashamed. Shame required energy. She didn't have it.

She unscrewed the top with a twist that was too practiced to be new, took a swallow that didn't burn so much as settle, and let her shoulders drop an inch.

There. Something familiar.

The VCR hummed below the TV, steady and patient. Its little red display glowed like an eye that never blinked.

Alice leaned forward and pressed rewind.

The machine obeyed immediately, that low mechanical whir filling the living room in a way the house never did. The screen flashed blue, then static, then the image returned—color bleeding backward, motion collapsing into itself.

She pressed play.

Thomas again.

The upstairs hallway again.

His voice again—soft, almost conversational.

"You've been here all along."

The world did that thing it had started doing lately—like someone had reached over and turned the volume down.

Not gone. Not silent.

Just turned down enough that nothing pushed back.

Alice watched it happen, watched the dimness occupy the space between Thomas and the crack of her door, watched the tape cut to black at the exact same place it had before.

She didn't blink.

She pressed rewind again.

Watched again.

And again.

Each time, the same. No new angle. No hidden answer. No different outcome. Just proof. Just completion.

Her flask warmed in her hand.

She took another swallow.

When she finally pulled her eyes from the screen, her vision snagged on something she hadn't noticed before.

A VHS tape lay on top of the television—tilted slightly, like someone had set it there without care and never came back.

Alice stared at it.

The house did not react.

The VCR hummed, waiting.

Alice reached up slowly, like she was afraid the tape might vanish if she moved too fast. Her fingers closed around the plastic case.

It felt heavier than it should have.

She didn't read the label. She didn't trust herself to.

She pressed eject.

The VCR clicked, and Thomas's tape slid out partway, warm to the touch when she pulled it free.

She set it down on the floor beside her, a little farther away than she meant to.

Then she slid the new tape in.

The machine accepted it without hesitation.

Alice didn't realize she was holding her breath
until she pressed play and the tape responded immediately—no static, no delay, no argument.

The screen flickered.

Then steadied.

A timestamp appeared in the corner.

FEB 17, 2013 — 2:17 A.M.

And Alice saw herself under fluorescent hospital
light, hair plastered to her temples, face hollowed
out by pain and exhaustion—still smiling anyway,
like her body had been torn open and it had been
worth it.

The camera was too close. Angled wrong.
Someone filming with one hand like they weren't
sure they were allowed to.

Alice—young Alice—lay back against white pillows, eyes wet, cheeks damp, lips parted like she
couldn't decide whether to laugh or sob.

A nurse stepped into frame, practiced and gentle, and placed a newborn into Alice's arms.

Small. Red-faced. Wrinkled like an old man. Fu-
rious at the world.

Then he quieted, settling against her chest like
he recognized something.

Alice's mouth trembled.

"Oh," she whispered.

Not oh my God. Not thank you. Just oh—like her soul had been surprised by how much it could hold.

The nurse leaned in, smiling. "What's his name?"

Alice looked down at the baby like she was reading the answer off his skin.

"Jesse," she said, voice thin from everything she'd just survived. Then she tried again, stronger. "Jesse."

The nurse nodded. "Middle name?"

Alice blinked slowly, as if the name had been waiting behind her eyes the whole time.

"Thomas," she said.

The way she said it wasn't random. It landed like an anchor.

"Jesse Thomas Holloway." Alice swallowed, her throat working hard. "He deserves a good name," she added softly. "A bright name."

The baby made a sound that wasn't quite a cry—more like a complaint—and Alice laughed through tears, exhausted and radiant all at once.

The camera wobbled as whoever held it adjusted, like they were crying too.

FEB 17, 2014 — 2:17 P.M.

The next clip hit without warning.

A small apartment living room, sunlight spilling across cheap carpet. A single balloon drooped in the corner. A cake on a folding table, slightly crooked, candles already lit.

Just the two of them.

Alice held Jesse on her hip. He was chubby and fussy, cheeks full, hands grabbing at everything like he was determined to own the world.

"Okay," Alice said, smiling too hard. "Okay, baby —look."

She leaned him forward toward the candles.

"Yay! Make a wish!"

Jesse blinked at the flames like they were an insult. He fidgeted, squirming, trying to twist away.

Alice laughed, that bright laugh that tries to outrun how tired you are.

"I know, I know," she cooed. "You don't care. But I care."

She blew out the candles for him, cheeks puffing, and the smoke curled up in a thin ribbon.

"Yaaay," she said, clapping softly, like she was cheering for both of them.

The camera dipped and caught Alice's hand at the edge of frame.

A cup.

Not a big one. Not dramatic. Just something amber in plastic.

She took a sip without making a face, without acknowledging it.

Like it was part of the ritual.

Then she kissed Jesse's cheek—loud, playful— until he squealed and shoved her away with tiny angry hands.

Alice laughed again.

But her eyes stayed tired, even while she smiled.

FEB 17, 2018 — 2:17 P.M.

Sidewalk. Wind. A brighter day.

Jesse, five, wobbling on a bike with training wheels, knees high and awkward. Helmet too big. Smile too wide.

"Go, go, go!" Alice shouted, jogging behind him with one hand hovering near the seat like she couldn't trust the world not to steal him.

Jesse laughed, loud and fearless. "Mom! Watch!"

"I'm watching!" she called back, breathless and grinning. "I'm watching!"

He swerved, almost ate the pavement, corrected at the last second, and shrieked like the near-miss was the best thing that had ever happened to him.

Alice laughed so hard she had to bend over.

The camera caught her for a second—hair pulled back, face flushed, hand lifting something to her mouth while she tried to catch her breath.

A bottle this time.

Not hidden. Not explained. Just there.

She took a quick swallow, wiped her mouth with the back of her hand, and went right back to running after him.

"Okay—okay—slow down, Jesse!" she shouted, laughing as she chased him like the world was safe enough to play in.

FEB 17, 2025 — 2:17 P.M.

This clip looked sharper. Newer.

Jesse at twelve—taller, limbs too long, face still soft enough that childhood hadn't fully left it. He stood in the living room holding a video game console box like he didn't trust it was real.

Alice's voice was behind the camera, trembling with pride she was trying not to show.

"You earned it," she said. "You hear me? You earned it."

Jesse laughed, eyes bright. "I know! I know!"

He hugged the box to his chest like it was a trophy.

Alice stepped into frame for a second—just long enough for the camera to catch her expression.

She looked like someone who had been holding her breath for years and had finally been allowed to exhale.

Jesse bounced on his heels. "Can I set it up? Right now?"

"Yeah," Alice said, laughing. "Yeah, go—go, go!"

He sprinted toward the TV, already tearing at the packaging.

The camera followed him, jittery, catching the edge of Alice's hand as she reached down beside the couch.

A drink again.

More visible now.

Not celebratory. Not cute.

Necessary.

Alice lifted it, took a longer pull than before, eyes still on Jesse like she was drinking to keep her joy from breaking open into fear.

Jesse glanced back. "Mom?"

"I'm good," she said immediately, too quickly. Then softened it. "I'm good, baby. I'm just... happy."

Jesse smiled and went back to his console, humming to himself.

Alice stayed behind the camera.

And for a second—just a second—her smile faltered like her body remembered that happiness isn't a shield.

The clip cut.

Alice didn't realize she was crying at first.

It wasn't loud. There was no sharp intake of breath, no sound that demanded attention. Just warmth on her face that didn't belong there, gathering at her chin before falling away.

She wiped at her cheek with the back of her hand and stared at the screen, confused by the moisture left behind.

"Oh," she whispered.

Her chest tightened suddenly, without warning, like something had finally broken loose after being held in place too long. The feeling came fast and heavy, pressing in from all sides.

"I'm sorry," Alice said.

She didn't know who she was saying it to.

The room felt smaller now. Closer. The television's glow seemed harsher, less forgiving. Her hands shook as she reached for the flask again, fingers fumbling at the cap before she managed to twist it open.

She drank.

It didn't help.

Her breath hitched, and this time the sound did escape her—thin, involuntary, like a crack in glass.

"I tried," she said, voice breaking. "I really did."

The tape kept playing.

Or rather—something else did.

The image glitched.

For a split second, the screen fractured into static, sound warping just enough to be noticed. Then it steadied again, resolving into a new frame.

A different timestamp appeared in the corner.

NOV 24, 2025 — 11:24 P.M.

Alice froze.

The camera was moving.

Not handheld this time—mounted. Shaking slightly with motion. Streetlights streaked past in uneven flashes of white and orange. The sound was wrong, too loud and too hollow at the same time—engine noise bleeding into itself, the hum of tires on wet pavement.

Alice's breath caught painfully in her throat.

"No," she said, barely audible. "No, no—"

The road curved sharply.

Headlights flared.

For a moment, the world seemed to pull inward,

like everything was being drawn toward a single point.

Then—

The sound dropped.

Not all at once.

Just enough.

For a moment, the world felt slightly muted—

not gone, not silent,

just turned down enough that nothing pushed back.

The image blurred violently. Light smeared across the screen. A sudden impact sent the camera skidding, the angle collapsing sideways.

Alice gasped.

Her stomach lurched hard enough that she doubled over, one hand slapping against the floor as if to steady herself. The taste of metal flooded her mouth.

"Oh God," she choked.

The screen kept showing it.

Glass. Twisted light. A shape that might have been a door, or a road sign, or nothing at all.

Alice retched, the sound sharp and wet in the quiet room. She barely had time to turn her head before her body betrayed her, emptying itself onto the floor beside her.

Her hands trembled violently as she pushed herself back, sobbing now, breath coming in broken pulls that hurt her chest.

"I killed him," she whispered.

The tape didn't respond.

The timestamp stayed fixed in the corner.

11:24

The number burned.

Alice pressed her palm flat against her mouth, tears streaming freely now, her vision swimming as the footage continued without mercy.

The loop had tightened.

And it wasn't done yet.

The image steadied.

The camera angle was wrong now—tilted, low, half-buried against something dark. A dashboard, maybe. Shattered glass glittered across the frame, catching light in dull, broken points.

Smoke drifted through the interior of the car.

Someone shouted.

A door was pulled open, metal screaming as it bent. Cold air rushed in, loud and sharp against the muted interior sound.

"Ma'am—hey—ma'am, can you hear me?"

Hands reached into frame. Not gentle, but careful. Urgent without panic. Someone gripped her arm, then loosened it when she flinched.

"You're okay," a man said. "You're okay. We've got you."

The camera jolted as Alice was pulled sideways. The world lurched violently, light flooding the frame in harsh white as she was lifted out of the car.

The sound dipped again—not gone, just distant. Like everything was happening behind glass.

Her feet hit the pavement hard. She cried out, the sound thin and delayed. Someone wrapped an arm around her shoulders, steadying her as her legs buckled.

"Easy—easy," the man said. "I've got you."

She turned her head suddenly, frantic.

"Jesse?" she said. "Where's—where's my son?"

The camera swung with her movement.

The car filled the frame.

Or what was left of it.

The front end had folded inward completely, metal crushed and layered in on itself like it had been compressed by force rather than impact. The windshield was gone. The engine compartment no longer existed as a distinct shape.

The passenger side was worse.

The seat was still there. The belt still fastened. The airbag hung deflated and torn, collapsed inward on itself like it had finished its job and failed anyway.

There was no movement.

No sign of Jesse inside the car.

Alice made a sound that didn't fully form into a word.

"No," she whispered. "No—no—"

Something clattered to the ground near her feet.

The camera dipped instinctively.

Her flask lay on the pavement, rolling once before coming to rest against the curb.

Alice reacted immediately—too quickly.

She lunged, nearly falling, fingers closing around the metal before anyone else could notice it. She clutched it to her chest as she straightened, breath ragged, eyes wild.

"Hey," the man said softly. "It's okay. You're safe."

She looked up at him, shaking.

"Where is he?" she asked again. "Please. Where is my son?"

The man hesitated.

Just a second too long.

"My older boy—he got him out," the man said carefully. "He was in the front with you. We—he pulled him free right away."

Alice nodded rapidly, relief crashing through her so hard it made her dizzy.

"Okay," she said. "Okay. That's okay."

The man's expression didn't change.

"He's... over there," he said, gesturing down the road. "We laid him on a blanket. Just until the ambulance gets here."

Alice followed his gaze.

The camera followed too.

A few yards away, on the shoulder of the road, a blanket lay spread out against the cold pavement. A small shape rested on top of it—still. Too still.

Someone knelt beside it, unmoving.

Alice stopped breathing.

"Can I see him?" she asked.

The man tightened his grip on her shoulder, just slightly.

"You can," he said. "But—"

The sound dropped out again.

Not silence.

Just enough.

For a moment, the world felt slightly muted—

not gone, not silent,

just turned down enough that nothing pushed back.

The image blurred as Alice staggered forward, the camera struggling to keep up, her breath coming in shallow, uneven pulls.

The blanket filled the frame.

Jesse didn't move.

The tape stuttered.

Then froze.

The timestamp burned in the corner of the screen.

11:24

The image held.

And held.

And held

Alice screamed.

"I killed him."

The words tore out of her chest raw and unfiltered, ripping through the thin quiet of the room.

She staggered backward from the television, shaking her head violently like she could dislodge what she'd just seen.

"I killed him," she sobbed. "I killed him. I killed him!"

Each repetition came louder, more desperate, like saying it enough times might finally make it stop being true.

Her hands fumbled blindly for the flask.

She didn't drink this time.

She hurled it.

The metal struck the television dead center with a sharp, cracking sound. The screen exploded inward, glass splintering and collapsing in on itself. The image vanished in a burst of white and black, the timestamp shattering with it.

The room went dark.

Alice dropped to her knees where she stood.

The force left her all at once, like something had finally let go. She folded forward, arms wrapping around herself so tightly it looked painful, fingers digging into her shoulders as if she were trying to hold herself together by sheer will.

Her cries came uncontrolled now—deep, broken sounds pulled from somewhere below language. Not words. Not thoughts. Just grief, pouring out of her in heaving waves that left her gasping for air.

She rocked there on the floor, hunched and shaking, forehead nearly touching the carpet, clutching herself like she was afraid she might disappear if she didn't.

The television stayed broken.

The house stayed quiet.

Nothing came to help her.

Alice stayed on the floor for a long time.

She didn't know how long. Time had stopped behaving like something she could measure. Her body ached in places she hadn't registered yet—throat raw from screaming, chest tight from crying so hard it felt bruised from the inside.

The television lay shattered in front of her, its screen spiderwebbed and dark. A faint electrical smell hung in the air. The VCR hummed uselessly beneath it, still powered, still waiting.

Alice didn't look at it.

She curled in on herself instead, arms locked tight around her ribs like she was holding something in place. Her crying softened eventually—not because the pain eased, but because her body ran out of strength to sustain it.

Her breath came in shallow pulls.

"I can't do this," she whispered to no one. The words barely made it past her lips. "I can't—"

Her voice broke again.

She wiped her face with the sleeve of her hoodie, smearing tears and snot without caring how it looked. Her hands trembled as they fell into her lap, useless now.

She needed someone.

The thought arrived fully formed, sudden and desperate.

Anyone.

Alice crawled across the floor on her knees and reached for her phone where it lay near the couch. Her fingers fumbled with it, slick with sweat, pressing the wrong button twice before the screen finally lit up.

The brightness hurt.

She squinted at it, vision swimming, contacts blurry with tears. The screen steadied enough for her to make out a name.

Jared

Her thumb hovered over it.

He probably wouldn't answer.

It was late.

She didn't even know what she would say.

Her chest tightened again, panic building fast and hot.

"I just need to hear a voice," she whispered. "Please."

She pressed call.

The phone rang once.

Twice.

Alice hugged it to her ear like it might slip away if she didn't hold on tight enough.

"Jared?" she said immediately, voice cracked and too loud. "Jared, it's me."

She swallowed hard, breath hitching.

"I—I don't know what to do," she continued, words tumbling out unevenly. "I just... I needed to call someone. I needed—"

The line stayed open.

Too open.

"Jared?" she said again, quieter now.

There was no response.

No background noise. No breathing. No accidental sound that suggested a person on the other end.

Just space.

Alice pulled the phone away from her ear and stared at the screen.

The call timer wasn't moving.

There was no indication it was connected at all.

Her stomach dropped.

She brought it back to her ear anyway, stubborn, desperate.

"I'm sorry," she whispered. "I'm sorry if I'm bothering you. I just—"

The call ended.

The screen went dark.

Alice stared at it, waiting for something to change. A missed call notification. A voicemail icon. Anything that would prove she hadn't imagined it.

Nothing appeared.

Her hand shook as she lowered the phone to her lap.

"Oh," she said softly.

Not surprise.

Recognition.

Alice leaned back against the couch, eyes unfocused, phone still clutched in her hand like it was the last solid thing left in the room.

She didn't cry again right away.

She just sat there, empty and exposed, realizing too late that even reaching out had become part of the loop.

And somewhere in the house, something continued—

not moving forward,

not ending,

just running.

The phone stayed dark in her hand.

Alice let it slip from her fingers. It landed facedown on the carpet with a dull sound that barely registered.

She leaned her head back against the couch and closed her eyes.

That's when she heard it.

Not thunder. Not rain.

Just the low, distant roll of something moving far away—so far it might've been imagination if she hadn't felt it too. A subtle pressure change. The air shifting in a way her body recognized before her mind did.

She opened her eyes.

The room looked the same. The shattered television. The quiet hum beneath it. Nothing out of place.

Outside, the wind picked up.

Branches brushed faintly against the side of the house, a soft scraping sound that blended with the house's other noises. Somewhere down the street, something loose rattled once, then settled.

A brief flash of light passed through the living room window—dull and distant. Not lightning yet. Just the sky adjusting.

Alice didn't move.

The first drop of rain struck the glass.

Then another.

Then enough to be heard.

The storm didn't arrive all at once. It gathered. Organized itself. Patient.

Alice stayed where she was.

9

THE ONE WE MISSED

The storm arrived all at once.

Thunder cracked overhead, close enough to shake the walls, the sound deep and physical like something slamming its weight against the house. The lights flickered violently, dimming, flaring, then settling into an unsteady glow that made the room feel unfamiliar.

Alice flinched.

Another thunderclap followed almost immediately, louder than the last. The windows rattled. Rain hammered against the glass now, no longer tentative, no longer gathering—fully committed.

Alice pressed her palms against the floor and pushed herself upright, heart racing. The sound was too much. The room was too open. The broken television sat dark and useless behind her, glass scattered like evidence she couldn't clean up.

"I can't—" she whispered, breath catching. "I can't stay here."

Another flash of lightning lit the house in stark white, every shadow snapping into place before dissolving again.

Alice turned toward the hallway.

Her feet carried her before she finished the thought.

The upstairs felt colder than the rest of the house. Each step of the staircase creaked beneath her weight, the sound swallowed quickly by the storm. Thunder rolled again, longer this time, stretching until it felt less like noise and more like pressure.

She reached the landing and paused, hand braced against the wall.

The door at the end of the hall stood open.

Her childhood bedroom.

Alice swallowed and stepped inside.

The room was smaller than she remembered. The furniture was wrong—too old, too still. The bed sat against the far wall, blankets folded neatly, untouched. Everything smelled faintly of dust and something else she couldn't place.

Lightning flashed again, illuminating the room in sharp, frozen detail.

Alice crossed the floor and climbed onto the bed, pulling the blankets around herself like muscle memory had taken over. She curled onto her side, knees drawn tight to her chest, the storm roaring around the house as if it were circling it.

"This used to help," she whispered.

It didn't.

The thunder grew louder. Closer. The lights

flickered again, then steadied just long enough to make the next flash of lightning feel cruel.

That's when she felt it.

Not a sound.

Not movement.

Presence.

Alice stiffened beneath the blankets, breath shallow and fast. Her eyes fixed on the doorway, heart pounding so hard it hurt.

Slowly, she pulled the covers down from her face.

Something stood at the threshold.

Just a shape at first. Small. Still. The silhouette of a child, framed by the dim hall light behind it.

Alice's breath hitched.

"Jesse?" she whispered.

The shape didn't move.

Tears spilled down her face as relief crashed through her, sudden and desperate. She didn't question it. She couldn't afford to.

"Jesse," she said again, louder now, her voice breaking. "Baby?"

The silhouette lifted its arms.

Inviting.

Alice threw the blankets aside and slid off the bed, bare feet hitting the floor. She took a step toward the doorway, arms trembling as they lifted halfway in return.

Another step.

Then she stopped.

Something was wrong.

Not in the way fear announces itself. Not sharp. Not sudden.

Familiar.

The world did that thing again—

the volume dipping, the storm's roar dulling, the thunder losing its edge like it had been padded from the inside.

Alice's chest tightened.

She'd felt this before.

Her father's study.

The hallway.

The tapes.

"No," she whispered.

Lightning split the sky outside, bright enough to turn the room white.

And for a fraction of a second, she saw it clearly.

The silhouette wasn't a child.

It was vast—too tall for the doorway, its shape folding in on itself unnaturally. Its surface wasn't solid but layered, made of drifting strands and dark matter that moved without wind. Vein-like tendrils stretched outward, trailing across the floor and walls, not touching, not quite there.

Its center was hollow.

A void that pulled at the edges of the room, bending light toward it, swallowing detail. The stars embedded within it shimmered faintly, distant and uncaring, like something wearing the memory of a sky.

Alice stumbled back, terror finally cutting through the fog.

"Oh," she breathed.

Recognition hit her all at once.

This is what it was.

This is what took him.

This has been here the whole time.

The entity didn't move.

It didn't need to.

Alice opened her mouth to scream.

No sound came out.

The storm vanished. The thunder. The rain. The house itself—all of it dropped away as the world fell silent, not gone, not erased, just turned down until nothing resisted.

The void expanded.

And in the blink of an eye—

Alice was gone.

EPILOGUE

The television murmured in the background. Jared sat on the couch with one arm draped along the back, half-listening as a news segment played. A woman leaned against his shoulder—someone he'd been seeing casually. Her attention drifted in and out, more focused on her phone than the screen.

"...continuing to monitor anomalous energy signatures..."

The camera cut to a man standing in front of a neutral backdrop. Gray at the temples. Composed. Careful with his words.

"Dr. Arthur Adams," the lower third read.

"...what we're seeing," Adams said, "are localized events appearing without pattern. No geographic consistency. No demographic trend. The only constant is duration."

Jared glanced up.

"These signatures linger for approximately three days," Adams continued. "Then they dissipate. Whatever they are, they don't move. They don't spread. They remain... present. Until they're gone."

The woman shifted slightly. "This sounds fake," she murmured.

Jared didn't respond.

"We're also investigating a possible correlation with unexplained disappearances," Adams said. "Cases where individuals vanish without evidence of struggle, and—more concerning—without sustained memory among those closest to them."

The anchor leaned in. "You're saying people forget?"

Adams hesitated.

"I'm saying," he replied carefully, "that in many of these cases, loved ones report a sense of absence without context. Emotional recognition without narrative recall. As if something was... missed."

The segment cut to B-roll. A map. Scattered points blinking briefly before fading out.

Jared's phone vibrated in his hand.

He frowned and looked down.

One missed call.

One voicemail.

The timestamp read 11:42 PM.

Jared's brow furrowed. He didn't remember the phone vibrating that late.

"That you?" the woman asked, glancing over.

"No," Jared said automatically. Then paused. "I don't think so."

He tapped the notification.

The room felt quieter immediately, like the television had lowered itself without being asked.

A woman's voice came through the speaker.

Soft at first. Unsteady.

"Hey... it's me."

Jared's chest tightened.

"I just—" the voice continued, breath hitching. "I just wanted to say... I tried. I really tried."

There was a pause. A faint sound in the background. Wind, maybe. Or nothing.

"I didn't mean to," she said. "I didn't mean to. I killed him."

Jared swallowed.

The voice shifted—sharper now. Angrier. Looping.

"I killed him. I killed him. I killed—"

The recording cut off mid-word.

Silence rushed in to fill the space.

Jared stared at the phone, thumb hovering uselessly over the screen.

The woman beside him leaned forward. "Who was that?"

Jared opened his mouth.

Nothing came out.

He searched himself for a name. A face. A reason the sound of that voice felt like it had reached somewhere deep and old inside him.

"I... don't really know," he said finally.

Then, quieter—more to himself than to her:

"But I feel like I do."

The television continued talking.

Outside, the night stayed still.